THE DEAN CURSE CHRONICLES

STEVEN WHIBLEY

Published in 2013 by Steven Whibley Publishing
Victoria, British Columbia
www.stevenwhibley.com

Publisher: Steven Whibley
Editing: Mahak Jain; Devin Govaere
Copyediting: Jon VanZile; Mary Thompson
Cover Design: Pintado (rogerdespi.8229@gmail.com)
Interior Layout and Design: www.tammydesign.ca

Library and Archives Canada Cataloguing in Publication

Whibley, Steven, 1978-
      Glimpse / Steven Whibley.

(The Dean Curse chronicles)
ISBN 978-0-9919208-1-5 (eBook)
ISBN 978-0-9919208-2-2 (bound).--ISBN 978-0-9919208-0-8 (pbk.)

      I. Title. II. Series: Whibley, Steven, 1978- . Dean Curse chronicles.

PS8645.H46G55 2013   jC813'.6   C2013-901948-0

This book is dedicated to my sister, Lisa, and my niece, Morgan, for braving the very first draft; to my editor, Mahak Jain, for tirelessly pushing me to make this story the very best it could be; to my son, Isaiah, who is only two and won't be reading this book for years, but who is a constant source of inspiration; and finally, and with great love, to my wife, Corene, who encouraged me to write when it was all just a dream.

– Steven Whibley

GLIMPSE

THE DEAN CURSE CHRONICLES

STEVEN WHIBLEY

CHAPTER 1

I'm cursed.

I know, I know, you don't believe me. Well, I didn't believe it was possible either... until the guy who cursed me came along. So go ahead and think I'm nuts. But one of these days, we might just meet up and then... well, you'd better believe whatever I say to you. Your life will absolutely depend on it.

My name's Dean. Dean Curse. Yes, I see the irony in my name, no need to mention it. I was ordinary once. I tolerated school and did all right in math, but I was no Stephen Hawking. I liked soccer and read mostly comics. My favorite TV show was *Survivor*. I watched it all the time. I planned to be on it and win when I turned eighteen. Of course, none of that matters anymore because like I said, I'm cursed.

It started a few days before my fourteenth birthday.

I gulped down a spoonful of cereal and tapped one

of the jars on the table. The moth inside twitched.

"Don't touch that!" Becky, my bigmouthed little sister, ordered. If being annoying was an Olympic event, she'd be wearing a gold medal.

"Why do you have all these jars of bugs?"

Becky closed her eyes and sighed. "I'm going to entomology camp this year, duh. I need specimens for my project."

"Entomology camp? Why can't you just play with dolls like normal girls?"

"I *am* a normal girl. Just because *you* don't know how to be normal doesn't mean no one else does."

"Yeah, whatever." I lifted another spoonful of cereal and paused. Becky glared across the counter at me, no doubt wondering how she could fit me into one of her jars. "Don't you have some rat traps to set or something?" I asked.

Every few months, Becky adopted a new hobby, each one more disturbing than the one before. A few months before, she had started to collect animal bones as if she were a junior paleontologist. The time before, it was rusted pieces of metal. The more rust, the better. My parents only made her stop after I stepped on one of her rusty scraps and had to get a tetanus shot. Now, for the past six months, she'd been obsessed with all things that creep or crawl. Whatever she said, she was *not* a normal eleven-year-old.

Becky glared at me. "Rat traps?"

"For your *project*."

"You're such an idiot." She pulled the jars away from me. "En-to-mo-lo-gy. As in the study of insects. Not rodents." She lifted her chin. "I'm supposed to bring fifty specimens. You're looking at numbers thirty-seven, thirty-eight, and thirty-nine."

Number thirty-nine looked like a twig with legs, and I was kind of disturbed that insects like that actually existed. "Why aren't they moving?"

"Gee, I wonder," Becky mocked. "Maybe because they're dead?"

"You *killed* them?"

"Of course I killed them. How else am I supposed to pin them to the board?"

"You kill them, then you pin them to a board? You're a sick kid, you know that?"

Just then, Mom walked into the kitchen, pulled up a stool, and started watching me eat my breakfast as if I were competing for a prize or something. I half expected her to cheer when I scooped up my next bite.

"Fourteen already. Wow!" Her smile widened. "It feels like just yesterday that I was giving you a bath in the kitchen sink."

"Argh!" Becky pushed her bowl of cereal away.

"Thanks, Mom. Now I can't eat, and I probably won't go near the sink for the rest of my life."

I rolled my eyes. "My birthday isn't until Tuesday, Mom."

"I just can't believe my little boy is so grown up."

"Please promise me you won't make comments like that when my friends are here."

"What friends?" Becky said. "You don't *have* any friends." She grimaced as she placed her bowl in the sink, and then jumped back as if it were a bomb moments away from exploding. She turned and glared. "Why did you have to bathe that troll in here?"

"I have friends," I said, ignoring the whole troll jibe.

"Who? Colin? Lisa?"

"Yeah... "

Becky laughed as she gathered up her jars of death. "Who else is coming? You can't count imaginary friends."

I did know other people who wouldn't mind coming, but unlike Becky, I didn't like being the center of attention. It made me nervous, like I was being tested or something. That was why I had only invited Lisa and Colin, my best friends since second grade. That wasn't something my sister would understand, though, and I could see by her pasty sneer that she was preparing to fling more insults, so I played the one card that would end the conversation.

"Nice hair."

That was all it took. Becky's dark hair stood up around her pale face as if she'd just been electrocuted. It was as if her frizzy hair was her kryptonite, the one thing she felt so self-conscious about she could hardly bear it. Her face flushed and her eyes started hurling battle-axes.

"Well... well... you're a dork, and you have too many freckles. And... and... *your* hair looks like you just rolled out of bed!"

"I *did* just roll out of bed."

Mom pursed her lips and shook her head at me.

"What? All I said was that she had nice hair." I looked back at my sister. "I happen to like the I've-just-been-struck-by-lightning look. It suits you."

Becky let out a frustrated yell and stormed out of the kitchen. I counted to three before I heard the door to her room slam shut.

"That wasn't very nice, Dean," Mom said.

I shrugged. "It's the only way to get her off my back."

Mom poured herself a cup of coffee. I could feel her scrutinizing me, but I didn't turn around. "Maybe you should invite other people," she said finally. "Colin and Lisa are great, but you should give other kids a chance to get to know you too."

I took a deep breath and forced it out before replying. "I have other friends."

"I'm sure you do, Dean, but when's the last time you hung out with them?"

"All the time, Mom. Colin and Lisa just happen to be my *best* friends."

She gave me a *"Sure, I believe you"* look. "Be nicer to your sister, okay? Don't tease her about her hair." She walked over and kissed me on the forehead. "Now go get ready for school. Your father had to go in early today, but I'll drive you guys on my way to work."

Fifteen minutes later and only ten minutes before the first bell at school rang, Becky was still locked in the bathroom trying to tame her hair.

"Snails move faster," I grumbled.

Mom shrugged helplessly. I knew my sister, and I knew she was going to stay locked in the bathroom until I'd be late even with a ride from my mom. The only way I wasn't going to be late was if I walked—or ran, as the situation required. I threw my bag over my shoulder and headed out the door. Outside, the sky was clear and the air balmy with the first real heat of June. Summer vacation wasn't far off, I remembered with a smile, and then I sped down the street.

I stopped running a block away from the school, slowing to catch my breath. I checked my watch. Five minutes before the first buzzer! There was no way I could make it unless I took a detour. I ducked through an alley behind a strip mall.

And froze.

Two men, one roughly the size of a giant ape and the other tall and lanky, were stomping on a large mound of garbage heaped up against a rusted chain-link fence. It wasn't until I heard the garbage moan that I realized they were kicking a man who was crumpled on the ground and grunting with each strike.

My instincts told me to run, but my feet wouldn't listen. Instead, I did something else—something really, really stupid. I reached into my back pocket and pulled out my wallet. It was blue and had the Detroit Red Wings logo on the front. It looked nothing like a cell phone, but I held it to my ear and yelled, "I'm calling the cops!"

The two men spun and glared down the alley at me. Probably only a second or two passed, but even that felt too long—I tensed and wondered if they'd come after me next. Instead, they tore off in the opposite direction.

I slowly walked to the man on the ground. His filthy clothes were torn to ribbons and soaked in blood, and he was covered in garbage that had no doubt come from the overturned bin a couple feet away. A brown leather bag dangled from his shoulder. He rolled onto his back. Blood cascaded from a gash above his right eye and his nose was at an unnatural angle to the rest of his face.

My stomach lurched at the stench of him. I swallowed

back a mouthful of puke and helped him sit up against the fence.

"What's going on back here?" a nervous voice yelled from the end of the alley.

A skinny kid wearing an orange convenience store uniform gaped at us. He had a baseball bat in his hand but looked far too scared to use it.

"Call an ambulance!" I shouted. "And the police."

The beaten man coughed, spraying my Green Day T-shirt with specks of blood. He opened his mouth and tried to speak but only managed to mouth a word that I couldn't make out.

"Don't try to talk," I said. Sirens sounded in the distance. "You're going to be—"

His eyes suddenly widened to the size of doorknobs. He grabbed my shirt and pulled me close. I could feel his breath on my ear as he rasped a single word.

"*Glimpse.*"

And then his eyes closed and his head drooped. "Hey!" I yelled. But it was no use. He was unconscious. Only the sound of breath gurgling in his chest remained. And as for me... I didn't know it yet, but after that I'd never be the same.

CHAPTER 2

The ambulance arrived first, followed by four police cruisers. The paramedics took the man away on a stretcher—he was still unconscious and barely alive by the looks of it—while the police blocked off the alley with yellow crime scene tape. The officers wanted to ask me some questions, so I gave up any hope of making it to my first class. I described the men as best I could: big, burly, and mean-looking. "You might want to check if any large animals recently escaped from the zoo," I said, hoping a bit of humor would stop me from trembling.

One of the officers nearby gave a chuckle, but the one taking my statement looked stoic. "Zoo? Why would you say that? Did you hear them say something about the zoo?"

"What? No. I'm just saying they were big. Like animals. But they weren't animals." He just stared at me, so I added sheepishly, "They were people."

The officer sighed and pointed back down the alley. "Which way did they go?"

"Left," I said. "They went left."

An officer looking over the scene for clues pointed at a broken window facing the alley. "Wrong place at the wrong time," he said. "Looks like those men were trying to break in. I bet the man you helped interrupted them. Thieves aren't big on leaving witnesses." He jotted down a couple more notes and added, "There's been a string of break-ins around here this past week. I bet it's the same men."

I shuddered. A couple minutes earlier and it would've been me who interrupted the break-in. *I* might have been the one getting carted off on a stretcher.

Despite my protests, an officer—the one who had understood my warped sense of humor—insisted on calling my mom. I reddened as he talked to her, going on and on about my "act of bravery," until he finally handed the phone to me.

"Hi, Mom."

"Dean?" Her voice was sharp, and I imagined her clutching the cord of her phone as she paced in her office. "Are you okay, Dean?"

"I'm fine. It wasn't that big a deal."

"Are you hurt? The officer said you stopped some muggers from killing a man." She sounded skeptical. "Is that true?"

I snorted. Only Mom would entertain the idea that I had hired a police officer to give her a prank call. "It's kinda true. I didn't actually—"

"What were you thinking, Dean!? Putting yourself in harm's way like that. You could've been *killed*."

"Mom, just—"

Now Mom sounded shrill. "I'm coming down there right now. Just stay where you are and I'll be right there."

"Mom!" It wasn't often that I raised my voice to my mother, but the situation seemed to call for it. Plus, given what had just happened, I figured she'd forgive me. "I'm fine. Really. It wasn't that big of a deal. You don't need to come down here. Please, *don' t* come down here."

There was a lengthy pause. Mom seemed to be considering her options. "You promise you're okay?"

"I promise."

"Do you feel well enough to go to school?"

I might not have been the smartest kid on the block, but even I saw the opportunity. Since today was Friday, taking the day off would mean I'd get a three-day weekend. I turned my back on the officer and lowered my voice. "Maybe it would be nice not to see everyone today. I need to go home and get changed anyway."

"Why do you need to get changed?"

"Well, my shirt's ripped and—"

There was a sharp gasp from the other side of the phone and Mom's voice turned shrill again. "Ripped? Did the muggers attack you!?" Her voice reached a pitch that probably had every dog in the block barking.

"Mom, I'm fine. I'm not hurt. It's a small rip. I think I caught it on the fence or something. I'm not bleeding." I probably shouldn't have said anything, especially since my mom faints so easily. Dad and I always joked that her fainting was the reason the university covered the floor of her office with double-thick plush carpet even though all her colleagues got hardwood. "Okay, Mom," I said, raising my voice slightly and hoping some of what I said would make it through her hysteria and calm her down. "I'll just go home and get cleaned up. I'm fine. Don't worry. Bye."

I handed the phone back to the officer. "She, um, she said I should just go home and get cleaned up."

"I'll have someone drive you." The officer looked over his shoulder and gestured to one of his colleagues near the perimeter line.

"No, no, you don't need to do that," I said. We weren't that far from the school and I'd probably be spotted by someone I knew. Then everyone would want to know how I'd managed to hitch a ride with the police. Sure, I wanted to see the inside of a cop car, but not badly enough to deal with that kind of scrutiny. "I'm fine to walk. I only live a few blocks away. Honest, I'll be fine."

He shrugged, then handed me a card. "If you think of anything else, a better description of the men you saw, or if you remember anything later, give me a call."

"Sure." I slipped the card into my jeans pocket and ducked under the police tape.

I started feeling different right then. I don't know if I'd call it a sense of dread necessarily, but it was a general uneasiness that felt all the more urgent because my hands wouldn't stop shaking. At the time, I thought it was just strained nerves.

It wasn't.

I took the long way home, hoping a walk would calm me. It did. In fact, the more I thought about what had happened, the calmer I became and the more I started believing that I had actually done something remarkable. I'd stood up to two muggers. Thugs who might've had machine guns and machetes for all I knew. I'd risked my life for a stranger! I was a hero.

I grinned as I turned left on Fairfield Drive, stopping at Oakridge Mall. A mob milled around the doors to Gadget Emporium, one of the largest electronics chains in the country. Brightly colored banners announcing the grand opening flapped from flagpoles. An extra large banner was plastered across the red-brick structure, while on the rooftop a giant iPod-holding inflatable gorilla waved in time with the breeze and held a sign that promised *"Free giveaways! Today only!"*

When you're a kid who doesn't get an allowance, the lure of a free giveaway is kind of hard to ignore. Plus, what if the cosmos were rewarding me for risking my life? If so, I wasn't going to argue. And if that reward came in the form of some cool—and free—electronic device, all the better.

Determined, I cinched the straps of my backpack and pushed, ducked, and shimmied my way past one person after the next, buffeted back and forth until I stood at the front, my face inches from the double-wide glass doors.

Displays, advertisements, and colorful boxes covered with blinking lights lined the aisles and dangled from the ceiling. A handful of employees scuttled around, doing some last-minute shelf stocking.

"What time is it?" a woman asked over my shoulder. "It should be open now, shouldn't it?"

"Hey! Stop pushing," another voice said.

"Ouch!"

"Get off my foot!"

"C'mon already, open the doors."

The crowd pressed forward as an employee wearing a dark blue smock approached the doors from inside. He smiled, gave an excited wave, and inserted a key into the lock. Then he looked down at his watch and silently mouthed down the final ten seconds.

As soon as the key *clicked*, the crowd surged. But the automatic doors didn't open quickly enough. My shoulder caught the edge as I was shoved through, and I staggered to regain my footing only to get slammed against the floor. I managed to pull myself to the side before I was pulverized to lunchmeat.

Great, I thought. *I survive a couple muggers only to be killed by a mob of bargain hunters.*

A foot caught me in the ribs. As I started coughing, an arm reached around my chest, heaved me to my feet, and yanked me through the mob, away from the entrance.

"Jeez, kid, whaddaya think you were doing down there?"

"G... getting trampled, m... mostly," I gasped, rubbing the side of my chest. "Thanks for helping me," I managed.

"That's what I'm here for," he said, keeping his gaze fixed on the crowd. He wore a green Gadget Emporium golf shirt that was ripped and stretched, and he had a few scratches on his arms. I probably wasn't the first person he'd fished out of the mob.

A heavyset woman came barreling out of nowhere, and we both leaped back as she dove into a videogame display next to us. She emerged from the twisted cardboard a moment later with a triumphant scream and a copy of *Bounty Hunter III* clutched in her hands.

"What is wrong with these people?" I wheezed.

"When there's free stuff to be had, people go nuts," the guy said. "Are you gonna be all right?" He grimaced when I turned to him. "Ouch. You don't look so good." He gestured to my T-shirt. "Is that your blood? Do you want me to call someone for you?" He pulled out a cell phone from his pocket.

"Blood?" I glanced down at the spatter across my shirt, shivering as I remembered the man in the alley. "I'm fine. It's not my blood."

He cocked an eyebrow.

"Really. I'm not too hurt."

Another wave of shoppers closed in on the display. I dove left and he dove right. I heard a crash but thought it best not to waste time looking back. *So much for the cosmos.* I slid around the outer wall of the store until I ducked through a side exit.

CHAPTER 3

I groaned when I saw Mom's silver Volvo parked in the driveway and Dad's Jeep sitting behind it. I guess it was a bit much to expect she would've trusted that I was fine.

I trudged through the door and dropped my bag in the foyer. "I'm home!"

"Dean?" My mom's voice came from the kitchen, but my dad rounded the corner first. As soon as he saw me, his mouth fell open and moved wordlessly. He seemed to be having a tough time speaking.

"A... are you... look at your face," he finally blurted. I winced. I must've been banged up when I hit the ground face-first.

"Where is my little hero?" *Uh oh.* Mom pushed past my dad and, without missing a beat, screamed. "You said you were fine!" With what seemed like superhuman speed, she was next to me with my face in her hands, turning my head one way, then the next. "You said they didn't hit you, Dean. Your face is all bruised up!"

"Mom, it's not what you think. Let me explain."

"What's this?" She grabbed my shirt. "Is that—"

"Mom, it's not my blood."

"B... blood." The color drained from her face and her eyes rolled back as she slumped over. My dad must've seen it coming because he caught her before her knees buckled and lowered her to the floor. Yup. She was unconscious.

"Are you okay, son?"

I didn't have a chance to answer him. The vision—the first sign of my newly cursed state—couldn't have come at a less opportune time, but I think the universe has a really sick sense of humor sometimes, so of course that's exactly when it did come. My dad had barely finished his sentence when all the color suddenly drained from around me. The foyer walls, my dad's face, his clothing, everything simply muted to shades of gray, as if I had suddenly developed a special strain of colorblindness. I blinked rapidly, expecting the color to return. It didn't. Instead, a woman I was *sure* I'd never seen before appeared to my left.

At first, I thought my parents had company. I glanced at my dad and then back at her. I was about to say "Hello" and apologize for my mom when my sanity got a real kick in the biscuits. The woman seemed confused at first, but then her furrowed brow relaxed and her lips parted slightly, then a bit more. Soon they were curling back farther than lips were supposed to curl back. She dropped one shoulder while the other rose and shuffled forward a step, and then her body twisted more and more until she resembled a crumpled version of the letter S. I cringed at the sight of her, but I practically leaped into the air when she started screaming. Not an excited scream, like the one you might hear at a concert or on a roller coaster. No, this was the kind of scream that freezes blood, sends shivers up your spine, makes you pee your pants, and leaves one word pounding against the inside of your head: *Death*.

I staggered back in horror, caught my foot on my unconscious mother's head, and toppled to the floor. Then, as quickly as the strange woman had appeared, she was gone. The color melted back into the walls. For some reason, I could still hear her shrill scream, and it wasn't until I ran out of breath that I realized I was the one screaming. I scuttled back like a crab until my back hit the wall. "D... dad!" I gasped and pointed to where the woman had been standing. "W... what... w... who was that!"

You should know that my dad's a psychologist. He started his career in mental hospitals for the criminally insane, and when he figured he'd seen it all, he accepted a job at the university. So nothing freaks him out. Seriously. Nothing. I could go out and kill the neighbor's dog, skin it, and wear its head as a hat, and he'd calmly call it a *phase*. Okay, maybe he'd worry a little, but you get the idea. His expression was permanently fixed at cool and collected. But when I looked at him now, his eyes were the size of tombstones and his mouth gaped. Which is how I probably looked when I saw the woman. Except instead of focusing on where the woman had been, Dad's attention was on me.

He blinked twice before he shut his mouth and gave his head a quick shake. "What did you see, son?" He seemed to strain to keep his voice on an even keel.

"Th... that w... woman," I shouted. "You didn't see her? Y... you didn't h... hear her?"

Dad swallowed. "Did she tell you to do something, Dean?"

"W... what?" I looked from the void where the woman had been standing to my dad. "You didn't hear her screaming? You didn't see how twisted up she was?"

Dad gave an approving nod as if everything suddenly made perfect sense. He brushed his hands down the front of his shirt and straightened his tie, and just like that, his unsettled expression was gone. "Stand up, son."

I didn't move. I *couldn't*. I stared helplessly at my dad.

He walked over to me and helped me to my feet. My whole body shook. "It's okay, Dean. It's called PTSD. *Post-traumatic stress disorder.* I see it all the time in people who live through traumatic incidents: soldiers, people who have survived disasters, and quite often, people who have witnessed attacks."

"What are you saying? You think I *imagined* that

woman?"

He hesitated and placed a gentle hand on my shoulder as a flash of concern played across his face. "Hey, hey, don't worry. It's entirely normal, son. Sometimes PTSD manifests itself as hallucinations, auditory and visual, sometimes just as general anxiety. Don't worry. We can get past this easily."

"That was no hallucination," I insisted. "No way. That was something else."

"Dean." He leaned forward until our eyes were at the same level. "There was nothing there."

I glanced back at the floor. My mom shuffled into a sitting position and looked around the room, blinking.

"Welcome back, hon," Dad said. "Feeling better?"

My mom blinked some more. "I heard a scream. What happened?"

I shrugged.

"You should get changed, Dean," Dad said as he helped Mom up. "But come back down right after. We should talk some more." I started up the stairs as my dad added, "Don't worry, son. What you're experiencing is entirely normal and you'll be just fine."

Normal?

Screaming, twisted women who appear out of nowhere are normal? I think not.

Unfortunately for me, it turned out I was right.

CHAPTER 4

Thanks to my shaking hands and the fact that every creak and groan from the house made me jump, it took a while to change my clothes. But by the time I got downstairs, I had started to feel a bit silly about the whole thing. *Of course it was stress*, I decided. Though I figured it was more from getting trampled at the electronics store than anything else. My parents sat me at the kitchen table and grilled me for what felt like hours, but finally they were satisfied I was okay. My dad even believed I'd be fine without counseling. "But you're to keep me up to speed on how you're feeling, Dean," he insisted. "If I think you're not coping well, I'll want to set up some time with one of my colleagues. Got it?"

After screaming in the foyer, I wasn't in any position to defend my sanity. I agreed with a shrug, not really expecting that anything would come of it.

Once Dad had calmed down about my mental state, Mom insisted I see a doctor for my injuries. Immediately.

So we spent the rest of the day in the ER. We waited three hours to be told what I could have guessed on my own. I had a bruise on my rib and some cuts on my face, but other than being shaken up a bit, I was fine. "You did good today, Dean," Mom said when we pulled back into the driveway. "I'm proud of you for helping that man. A lot of people—a lot of adults—would have turned a blind eye."

"Thanks, Mom." She was starting to tear up, so I got out of the car as quickly as my bruised rib would allow, which turned out to be painfully slow. My sister was sitting at the kitchen counter playing with something inside a shallow black box when we walked in. She saw my face and flashed a wicked grin.

"Nice face. Dad said something about you getting beat up by a couple of girls behind a toy store or something? That's rough."

"You're funny." I walked to the fridge and poured a glass of orange juice. "Oh, yeah," I added, "Mom told me to warn you not to touch anything metal for a while. She thinks you have enough static electricity in your hair that a spark might cause the whole house to explode."

Becky said something back to me, but I never heard her. I only saw her mouth moving. For the second time that day, the color drained from around me. My pulse quickened, and I couldn't bring myself to swallow my mouthful of orange juice. I caught the slithering movement of something to my right and turned.

A large man with thin, dark hair had appeared out of

nowhere just behind Becky's shoulder. She seemed entirely unaware he was there. Suddenly, the man's face and posture deteriorated until he looked more like a zombie than a man. And that's when he screamed. The orange juice sprayed from my mouth and nose, and the plastic cup bounced on the tiled floor. The man was gone before the cup bounced a second time, and a wave of color righted the world around me.

I coughed and choked for several moments. When I finally looked back at Becky, she was white to the point of near transparency, and her eyes bulged. "W... what w... was that?" she asked.

My heart surged. *I knew I wasn' t crazy.* "You saw it." I pointed a shaking finger at my sister. "Don't mess with me, Becky. Did you actually see him?"

"H... him who?" she stuttered. "You look as if you've just seen a ghost."

"That's about how it felt," I muttered. I took a couple of slow breaths and grabbed a damp cloth to wipe up the mess I'd made.

"Are you... okay? What did you see?"

I used the cloth to wipe away some of the juice from my clothes before looking back at my sister. She leaned in over the counter.

"A man. He looked like a... I don't know. Like a zombie."

"You saw a zombie?" Now she seemed to be on the verge of laughter.

"Did I say that? I said he looked *like* a... " There was no point in continuing. Becky wasn't going to believe anything I had to say. I tossed the cloth into the sink. "What do you care anyway?" I marched out of the kitchen and up the stairs, wincing with each step but refusing to let the pain slow me down. I didn't stop until I slammed the door to my room behind me. I lowered myself onto my bed and pressed my palms against the sides of my head.

What's wrong with me? Am I going nuts?

The same two questions rattled around in my head until finally, and with great relief, I fell asleep.

I wish I could say that I stepped up, met this period of weirdness head-on, and worked through it. But I can't. When I woke up the following morning, I stayed in bed until noon, and then I really only left the room so I could get some food. Becky gave me a pretty wide berth for the first time in my life, so that was good, but the way she looked at me made me feel even more like a freak.

Colin and Lisa called—no doubt to see why I hadn't been at school on Friday—but I didn't take the calls.

Instead, I let Saturday pass with as few human interactions as I could manage: an awkwardly long talk with my dad about facing my PTSD with confidence and a dozen or so intrusions from my mom. But when Sunday morning arrived, I felt almost entirely normal. No additional hallucinations, no world turning gray, nothing. I actually felt well enough to eat breakfast with everyone.

"How are you feeling, Dean?" Dad asked. He looked up from the newspaper with a raised eyebrow.

"Better," I said truthfully. "I think this PTSD stuff might have run its course."

Dad looked doubtful, but nodded all the same. "I'm glad to hear it, son."

"Me too," Becky added. "It took me over an hour to get all that orange juice out of my hair. I'd prefer it if that never happened again."

"How's the bug collection coming along, Becky?" Dad asked.

Becky beamed. "Great. I'm sure I'll have the collection complete before camp, and it will probably be the best one too."

"I'm sure you're right, sweetheart," Dad said, "but don't rub it in the faces of your fellow campers. That's not the best way to make friends."

"Dad," Becky said, still smiling, "I'm not the kid you need to worry about when it comes to making friends."

My sister drove me nuts, but I felt better knowing that despite the hallucinations, she was treating me the way she always did. Still, I sensed something was wrong. There was a lingering nervousness, like everyone was trying really hard not to upset the crazy kid in the room. Not that I could blame them. If I saw one of them wig out the way I had, I'd probably go buy the straight-jacket myself. If it had been my sister, I'd have paid double to make sure it had a few extra buckles and maybe a hood.

Nah, I couldn't blame them. But I was fine. Better. *It'll take one more day*, I decided. *Tomorrow things will go back to normal.*

I told myself that again when I was finishing up some homework later that evening, deliberately ignoring the little voice in my head going on about "wishful thinking." *Tomorrow. Everything will be better tomorrow.*

CHAPTER 5

"Dean!"

I popped awake at the sound of my mother's voice and nearly fell out of my chair. I pulled at a piece of paper that was stuck to my face and realized I'd fallen asleep at my desk.

"I can't believe you're not awake yet!" my mom shouted from the doorway. "You have to be at school in"—she paused to check her watch—"thirty minutes. Now you're going to have to walk."

"W... what?" I blinked away the lingering confusion. I had somehow slept through my alarm too, which was beeping incessantly beside my empty bed. I dropped my head back down to the desk and exhaled. "What... what time is it?"

"Late, Dean," Mom said, pulling me up by my shoulders. "Very late." She turned me to face her. "How are you? Do you feel okay? Well enough for school?"

"I can't miss school, Mom. I'll fail my exams. Besides, I feel fine. Much better. I promise."

She rubbed her thumb under my eye. The sting

34

reminded me that it was still black. "Well, you still look like you were beat up by a gang or something. You're really going to be okay walking to school? If you're nervous about it—"

"Yes, Mom. Go. I'll be fine."

I grabbed a clean shirt and ran to the bathroom to shower. When I finished, the house was empty. I checked my watch: 8:15. I'd have to run, but I'd make it. I swung open the door and just about peed my pants right there on the porch. At first I thought I was having another hallucination. The woman had pasty skin and stringy blond hair. Mascara had clumped her eyelashes together as if she had taped two frozen spiders above her eyes, and she had the same blank expression the other hallucinations had in the moments before they screamed.

I jumped back and cringed.

"Are you Dean? Dean Curse?" the woman asked.

None of the other hallucinations had talked. I sighed in relief. "You're real."

"Pardon me?"

"Nothing. Sorry. Yeah, I'm Dean."

"Oh wonderful." She pulled out a notepad and pen. "I'm Regina Nelson from the *Gazette*." She cleared her throat and added, "Would it be okay if I interviewed you for a piece?"

"I'm not interested." I made my way onto the porch

and turned to lock the door. When I turned back to the reporter, I was greeted with the flash of a camera. "Wha... ?"

"How many muggers were there, Dean?" she asked, cutting me off and stuffing her camera into her handbag.

"T... two," I said. I gestured to her bag. "I don't want to be in the newspaper. Maybe you'd better interview the guy who was actually mugged."

She jotted a quick note and lifted an eyebrow. "I tried. He's not doing too well. And by the looks of your face, I'd say you didn't have an easy go of things yourself."

"It wasn't a big deal." I checked my watch: 8:25. "Darn it! I'm going to be late. I'm sorry, ma'am, but I have to go." I started running, but yelled over my shoulder, "Please don't use my name in the paper!" When I hit the end of the driveway, I broke into a sprint and made it all of five steps before the pain in my ribs slowed me to a light jog.

I gave up. I'd never make it.

The buzzer announcing the start of first period sounded from the PA just as I ran through the main entrance. I was late.

I inched open the door to my history class and tried not to notice when the room went suddenly silent and all eyes, including the ones belonging to Mrs. Farnsworthy, turned to me.

Mrs. Farnsworthy had to be at least fifty. She wore pleated skirts and solid-colored cardigans every day without fail, as if they were part of some dress code that only she knew about. She had a strange accent too, though you only really noticed when she said certain words, or when she got really upset. It always reminded me of the Soviet terrorists you see in old James Bond movies. She placed her hands on her hips and beat out a steady rhythm with her foot.

"Are you about ready to start, Mr. Curse?"

I gulped. I nodded as I sank into my chair.

"Good. Because we wouldn't want to inconvenience you by starting before you're ready."

"I'm sorry, Mrs. Farnsworthy. I'm only late becau—"

She waved a dismissive hand. "I don't want to hear it." She smoothed her hair with her palms and then returned them to her hips. "Maybe you can tell the class who fought in the War of 1812?"

"W... what?"

"1812, Mr. Curse. If you're going to come late to my class, I'll assume it's because you've already read the material and didn't think it necessary to come on time."

I had no idea what happened in 1812, but racked my brain to come up with something that wouldn't make me seem overly stupid. Colin was trying to whisper the answer from the desk behind me, but he sounded more like a hissing snake and only made me more nervous.

"Um... Vietnam and... uh... Korea?" I had a feeling that I was wrong when most of the class started laughing. In my defense, history just wasn't my thing. And plus, if your history teacher spoke like an ex-KGB spy, and she was glaring at you from across the room as if she were preparing to attack, you'd have a hard time answering too.

"Vietnam and Korea?" She cocked her eyebrow. "No, Mr. Curse, though perhaps the British and the Americans would have preferred it that way." Her expression soured. "One more interruption" — she raised a single finger as if I had no idea how many *one* was — "just one more and you'll have detention. Understand?"

I nodded and hunched in my chair.

"Where were you?" Colin whispered after Mrs. Farnsworthy returned to her lecture.

I shook my head and made a subtle gesture to tell him to be quiet.

"Okay, tell me later," he said. "But if she comes after you, remember to stop, drop, and roll. I'm pretty sure that's not just for fires. It works for crazy teachers too."

I coughed to stifle my laugh, only to have Mrs. Farnsworthy glare at me from across the room. Apparently, in her book a cough was enough to get me detention.

The thing is, I don't act out in class. I do as I'm told, and I follow the rules. I've only gotten detention twice in my whole life, and both those times were because of Colin. So what happened next was really out of character for me.

I was taking notes when it started. Like before, the color drained from the room and left it a dreary gray. I gripped the edge of my desk and drew a series of shallow breaths, not entirely sure if I was having another hallucination or a stroke, but praying desperately for the stroke. That's when things got even weirder. One second Mrs. Farnsworthy was droning on at the front of the class, and the next moment she was standing—*Whoosh!*—right next to me. Only not really, because... well, she was in both places, as if a twin had sprouted from her and transported magically across the room to kill me or, worse, to ask me another history question. Either way, for the second time today, I was on the verge of wetting my pants right then and there.

Shaking, I looked at the Mrs. Farnsworthy beside me. She had that same blank stare as the other hallucinations. Slowly, she started twisting and contorting her face. Her mouth widened and then, just like the others, she screamed. Shrieked is a better word, actually. She shrieked bloody murder. It seemed doubly worse than the other hallucinations because I knew her. Her features continued to distort, twisting like some human pretzel.

I reacted entirely on instinct. When you see something like that, no matter how hard you try, you can't think. Really, though, I only did what any other kid my age would've done. I leaped out of my chair and screamed too. I jumped back so hard that I hit Colin's desk and sent his books clattering to the floor.

Once again, the class was silent. My mouth dropped when I saw that Mrs. Farnsworthy's screaming twin had vanished. There was now only one of her standing at the front of the class.

She seemed to have forgotten all about history. I only realized that the room's color had returned when I noticed a slight hue of pink inching up her neck like a thermometer measuring rage. She clutched the front of her beige cardigan.

Mixed expressions crossed the faces of the rest of the class. Some kids seemed amused, others horrified. One thing seemed certain: I was once again the only one who had seen anything. I glanced back at Colin. His face was white and his mouth kept opening and closing as if he were a fish blowing bubbles.

"S... sorry, I... uh... I... " I searched through all the

excuses imaginable to explain my out-burst, hoping that I could come up with something before the pink hue, which had now crested Mrs. Farnsworthy's cheeks, climbed to the top of her head. "A rat," I said finally. "I saw a rat."

There were a few stifled gasps.

"A big one."

Reggie Sung was out of his chair before I finished my sentence. Reggie was the biggest baby in our grade. A few months ago someone had bumped into a light switch by mistake, and when the lights flicked back on three and a half seconds later, we found Reggie hiding under his desk. This time he sprinted to the back of the room and started hyperventilating.

He started a chain reaction. The gasps turned to shrieks as the other kids, particularly the girls, started seeing imaginary rats all over the place. Some even resorted to standing on their chairs. I would have laughed if I hadn't been so traumatized.

Mrs. Farnsworthy glanced at the floor to her right, then left, then slapped a nearby desk. "All right, all right," she said. "There are obviously no r—"

"There's one!" Colin yelled, pointing somewhere beside Mrs. Farnsworthy.

You wouldn't have thought anyone could move so fast or jump so high, but I blinked and she was on her desk, half crouched, peering over the edge at the floor below with a ballpoint pen clutched in her hand like a dagger. I heard wood crack when she stomped a foot on the desk to bring the class under control.

"Class!" she bellowed. "As we seem to have a... rodent... problem"—a visible shiver rolled up her spine—"you're all to go to the library, understand? Read chapters ten and twelve."

Just then, Jessica Barnes, seated just a couple rows in front of Mrs. Farnsworthy, shrieked, swatting frantically at something that had apparently attached itself to her leg about mid-calf. She leaped onto *her* desk only to shriek again. Mrs. Farnsworthy jumped in reaction, nearly falling off her desk in the process, and I swore I could hear the wood groaning in protest.

"Out!" she bawled. "Now!"

CHAPTER 6

No one spoke to me in the library, not even Colin, though he kept opening his mouth like he was about to say something. I could understand his confusion: he was the one who played pranks on teachers and students, not me.

The rest of the class kept whispering and nodding in my direction. If I didn't know any better, I'd say some of them looked impressed. But that was impossible. I'd caused the biggest scene ever. A few months back, Seth Brookfield, a kid from my algebra class, fell asleep and woke up calling for "Mommy." People still teased him about that, and my outburst was way worse. No, this was going to be bad. I was pretty sure I had set myself up for several weeks of relentless teasing. *What will it be?* I wondered. *Rat Boy? Rodent Kid? Screamy McScreamerson?* Okay, that last one probably wasn't going to stick.

But I had bigger things to worry about. I was still reeling from that hallucination. Something was very, very wrong with me. I even considered calling my dad and telling him to arrange a visit to the shrink.

When the bell for break finally rang, I couldn't get out of there fast enough. "You gonna tell me what happened in there?" Colin asked as students spilled out of the library and made for their lockers.

I wondered if I could play dumb. "What do you mean?"

"C'mon, Dean," Colin prodded. "You look like you've been clobbered by the girls' field hockey team, and you were screaming like you just saw your mom naked."

"Argh! Why do you always have to use such disgusting analogies?"

"Because I know that if I say something like that, the image will automatically jump into your head." Colin laughed. "You just thought about your own mom naked!"

"You're really disturbed, you know that?"

"Well, it sounded like you were the one disturbed. C'mon, spill already. It's not like you to make a scene. I mean, it was a genius way to get out of class early, and you had at least half the class fooled for a bit. Especially Mrs. Farnsworthy." He laughed and then got serious again. "But you were screaming for real and it wasn't about rats. Right?"

"It's a long story. I don't really know where to begin."

"Whaddaya mean? I figured you dozed off or something and were dreaming. That's not what happened?"

"No. Not exactly." I glanced over one shoulder and then the next. "What if I told you that one second I was listening to Mrs. F drone on about the British, and the next second I saw her standing beside me, clear as day, screaming like she was on fire?"

"She was on fire?"

"No. She was screaming *like* she was on fire. You know, like a crazy, terrified, soon-to-be-dead scream."

"Oh. Well, it would have been a better dream if you saw her burning alive." He looked up at the ceiling. "That would be one big fire."

"Argh. Are you even listening?"

We made it to our lockers, but instead of opening his, Colin shoved his history books into mine. He had his own locker, but it was filled with rotting food and dirty clothes. It made me seriously regret that my locker was next to his.

"Yeah, of course I'm listening. But the only one who screamed was you," Colin insisted. "Well, you screamed first, anyway." He turned and poked me in the chest. "So either you really saw her, you're on drugs, or you're nuts. I kinda hope you're nuts. I've always wanted a crazy friend."

"Mission accomplished," I muttered.

"Well, it was good timing anyway. We only had five minutes of lecture. That was great." He slouched against the lockers and watched the mob of students pass by. "You gonna tell me why you look so beat up?"

I was just about to tell him what happened when a heavily accented voice over my shoulder cut me off.

"Hey, Rat Boy."

I'd been expecting it and turned to see who would be the first to start what was sure to be a long line of name calling and sarcastic digs I'd be experiencing for the next week. When I recognized the culprit, though, I smiled. "Very funny, Lisa. Nice accent."

Colin nodded. "Yeah. You sound just like a drunken leprechaun."

She opened her mouth to speak but rocked back when I turned to face her. "God, Dean. What happened to your face? Is that why you weren't in school on Friday?"

"It's a long story."

She forced a smile. "Did it have anything to do with the vicious rodent attack that everyone's talking about?"

"It was awful," Colin said without missing a beat. "The beast was as big as a dog and came straight at Dean. Razor sharp teeth. No one thought he was going to survive."

"Must've been awful." She smiled and jabbed me in the shoulder. "You gonna be okay?"

"He will once he gets the image of Mrs. Farnsworthy out of his mind," Colin added.

"Oh gosh, did Colin make you think of her naked or something?" Lisa asked.

"No. But you just did!" Colin laughed. "Dean was thinking about her burning to death."

"What!" Lisa gasped. "That's a horrible thing to think about."

I closed my locker and turned to my friends. "I didn't see her naked and I didn't see her burning to death. Freaking out in class is not something I'll be living down anytime soon either."

"What are you talking about?" Lisa asked. "I heard the story from a group of girls in the hall and they were saying that it was brilliant."

"W... what?" I said. "They did?"

Lisa nodded. "Yep. No one's making fun of you. I think they've all realized by now it was just a prank." She stepped closer. "But I'd like to know what really happened."

I nodded. "Fine. But this is the last time I'm saying it, so just listen, okay?"

"Dean," Lisa said, reaching out for my arm, "you're shaking."

I could feel the sting of moisture behind my eyes and tried to blink it away. I was seeing things. Something was wrong with me, and I really didn't want my friends to think that I had totally lost it. At least Lisa and Colin wouldn't make fun of me—well, Colin might, but only until he realized I was serious; then he'd want to help. Since I had no idea what was going on with me, help was exactly what I needed. I cleared my throat.

"Hey, Dean. See any more imaginary rats?" There was no mistaking that sniveling voice: Eric Feldman, aka spoiled-rich-kid-who-buys-his-friends, aka douchebag extraordinaire, aka... well, you get the idea.

I turned slowly and watched Eric and his posse plow their way through the crowded hall. Students slowed and looked between me and Eric as though we were engaged in some invisible game of tennis. I sighed. I'd known Eric since he moved to Abbotsford in third grade. He had been a jerk even back then. Colin tricked him into eating yellow snow one winter and ever since we'd been at the top of his list of people to bully.

Colin stepped forward. "He thought he saw one, but it turned out to be your mom. I'm sure you can see how he confused the two."

Laughter erupted from the students who had stopped to watch, and their voices caught the attention of even more people until it seemed the entire school, or at least the entire ninth grade, was watching us.

Eric took a quick step forward but skidded to a stop when Colin clenched his fists and took a step of his own. Eric wasn't a tough kid. Actually, he was pretty much the definition of *prissy*. He even walked around on his toes most of the time, but that was probably because he was a bit smaller than the other kids in our class. Colin and I—even Lisa for that matter—could probably take him in a fight. Eric's best friend, Rodney Palmer, however, was a different story. Rodney was a Neanderthal goon who would frighten even a grown-up. Today, however, Rodney wasn't at school... Actually, he hadn't been in school for three days—a fact that had clearly slipped Eric's mind. Rumors had been circulating that Rodney had been picked up for shoplifting, which sounded pretty believable. Considering the type of thug he was, if there were rumors that Rodney was on the run after killing a cop, most everyone would have believed that too.

Rodney's absence, combined with a general distaste for Eric, spurred Colin's confidence. He seemed ready for a fight. Eric wasn't.

The crowd fell silent as Eric and Colin squared off against each other. Colin had a crooked smile and looked far too pleased. Eric, on the other hand, kept glancing over his shoulder at the gathering masses while he bit nervously on his lower lip.

"Get 'em, Colin!" someone shouted from the crowd. Another shout followed, then another, and before long, the whole crowd was egging the fight on. Some of the shouts were in support of Eric—who was looking more nervous by the second—but most were for Colin. No surprise there: Colin was one of those kids who was pretty much friends with everyone. This was good for me too, since that meant when he was around no one was looking at me.

I smiled. Colin was about to come through again. Eric Feldman getting his butt kicked was just the thing to make everyone forget about the whole rat debacle. I thought it was going to happen too, until the first buzzer sounded over the PA system and Mr. Shepherd came charging down the hall and commanded us all to class.

Lisa grabbed me by the shoulder. "We'll meet you here before lunch," she said as the crowd dispersed.

Second period was social studies, and it would have been the best place to sit and think about what was wrong with me. My teacher, Mr. Webber, was hands down the oldest teacher in the school. He had a bald head and age spots all over his face and arms. His wrinkled skin sagged like loose clothes. His hearing wasn't very good either, and as a result, he never asked the students many questions. He just stood at the front of the class pointing at various spots on his pull-down maps, entirely unaware of what was happening behind him.

It *would* have been a good place for me to drift into the background and gather my thoughts, if it hadn't been for the fact that Eric Feldman was in my class and he sat just a few desks away. After talking to Lisa, it seemed people thought I had done them a favor with the whole rat prank, but that didn't stop Eric from muttering things about invisible rats for the benefit of his posse. I was pretty sure he wanted the attention to shift away from how close he'd come to getting his butt kicked in the hall. It worked. Mr. Webber's lack of awareness enabled a barrage of notes to make their way to my desk, the bulk of which were signed by Eric as if they were pieces of artwork. One was a piece of scrap paper that he'd made to look like an official certificate announcing my insanity. Another was a picture of a giant rat eating a kid. My name was written with an arrow pointing to the kid, not that it was really necessary. The rest were more of the same.

By the time the buzzer sounded, the idea of spending another second in the school was too much for me to bear. Everyone was now eyeing me rather than ignoring me, and I felt as if I had a diaper strapped to my head.

Lisa and Colin were waiting by my locker when I got there.

"Look, I gotta go, guys," I said, not giving them a chance to speak first. "I'll see you tomorrow." I unlocked my locker and loaded my books into my bag.

"What do you mean?" Colin asked. "You're leaving?"

I nodded and slung my bag over my shoulder.

"Tell us what's going on," Lisa ordered. "What

happened to you, Dean?"

I was going to tell them. I even opened my mouth to speak, but then the image of Mrs. Farnsworthy flooded my head and I started wondering if I really was going crazy. If I had another hallucination, I didn't want it to be somewhere with so many witnesses. I was halfway down the hall and heading for the door before either one of them had a chance to say much else.

"I'll call you later," Colin yelled.

I didn't turn around. I suddenly felt smothered, as if a monster-sized blanket had fallen on me and threatened to stifle the very breath from my lungs. The only thing I could think of was getting outside.

Fresh air filled my lungs, and the feeling of suffocation was gone by the time I reached the corner. "I'm going crazy," I mumbled. I felt the urge to run, and that's exactly what I did. I ran as hard as I could, ignoring the pain in my ribs, until the school and everyone behind me fell away. Even more than the embarrassment, I had a feeling of dread that surged and twisted in my guts whenever I thought about Mrs. Farnsworthy. I wondered how fast I would need to run to lose that feeling.

CHAPTER 7

I cut through Mr. Utlet's yard and hoped the ornery old man wouldn't notice me. But of course I ran straight into him. I bounced back as if I'd just run into a brick wall, then winced and looked up. He was glaring down at me.

Mr. Utlet was one of those neighbors who looked both old and dangerous, as if he'd been an assassin in his youth and only retired to suburbia to throw off a hit squad out for revenge. He was on the small side of average, with short gray hair, a bristly face, and skin that looked like tanned leather. But despite his size, he came across as a giant. My dad said Mr. Utlet's tattoos—he had one on each forearm—were from his time in the army. Special Forces, no doubt. His eyes were what freaked me out the most, though. They were cold and dark, like the color of the sky just before a really bad storm.

"I told you not to cut through my yard, kid." Mr. Utlet's gaze flicked over my face and his expression shifted from angry to curious. No doubt he was wondering where all the bruises had come from. I wondered if he could see the fear in my eyes. Even worse, maybe he was like a dog or a bee, and he could *smell* fear. It wouldn't have surprised me one bit. "Sorry, sir," I said, dusting off my clothes, "it won't happen again."

He grunted and gestured for me to go.

I crossed the street in a flash, rushed through the front door of my house, and didn't stop until I was lying on my bed.

"What's wrong with me?" I groaned into my pillow. I pressed my hands to my head and closed my eyes.

The twisted image of Mrs. Farnsworthy screaming like a maniac—a dying maniac—played over and over in my mind until I couldn't keep my eyes closed for another moment. I tried to forget about the whole thing by studying my biology textbook, but it was no use. The moment I managed to get the image of Mrs. Farnsworthy out of my head, I instantly remembered what a scene I'd made and felt my cheeks flush with renewed embarrassment. I flipped a bit further through the book until the words started swimming off the pages and frustration got the best of me. I growled and threw it across the room. It hit my night table and knocked my alarm clock to the floor.

Get a hold of yourself! I took a breath, pushed myself to my feet, and paced in front of my bedroom window until I started getting dizzy. Then I plunked down at my computer and spent the next while surfing the

Internet for an explanation for what might be going on with me besides PTSD. I wasn't a psychologist, but the whole PTSD thing just didn't make sense. I hadn't been beaten up in the alley. I hadn't been attacked at all. No, it hadn't been fun to watch a man get beaten to pulp, but I didn't feel anxious when I thought about it. I wasn't worried the men were going to come and find me or anything. My hallucinations had to be the result of something else.

Exhaustion overwhelmed me, and I moved to my bed. *Just a quick nap*, I decided. I had barely finished the thought before I passed out.

At four-thirty, my mom knocked at the door and startled me awake. I hadn't heard her come home. "Colin's on the phone, honey. Do you feel well enough to talk?"

I cracked the door open. "Yeah. Thanks, Mom."

She handed me the phone and smiled one of those worried-mom smiles before heading down the hallway.

I took in a deep breath before speaking. "Hey, Colin."

"Hey, man, what's going on? Are you okay?"

"I'm fine, just tired, I think."

"So you're just seeing screaming faces because you're tired?" a girl's voice suddenly asked.

"Lisa?"

"Oh yeah, sorry," Colin said. "Lisa's on the line too."

I sighed. "You guys don't need to worry about me."

"Yeah right! You're either on drugs, schizophrenic, or, my personal favorite, *possessed*. I'm hoping you're possessed. That would totally explain the outburst in Mrs. F's class, plus I've always wanted to see an exorcism. You haven't been puking up green slime or crawling around on the ceiling, have you?"

I moved to the window. "You watch too many movies."

Colin chuckled.

"I think you're right... you're just tired. Stressed *and* tired," Lisa offered. "Are you feeling stressed out, Dean?"

"I'm fine." My parents already thought I was nuts. The last thing I wanted was my friends thinking the same thing. I tried to choose my words carefully. "There's"—I swallowed—"nothing wrong with me. I just... I don't know, maybe I've got a fever or something. That might explain all the hallucinations."

"Whoa," Lisa said. "*All* the hallucinations? As in more than one?"

I winced. "I guess there might have been a couple."

"Well, I still think it's stress." Lisa sounded less convinced, but I appreciated her effort.

"I don't," Colin said. "I still think he's possessed." I could hear the smile on his face.

The corners of my mouth twitched, and the tension

in my shoulders slackened. Colin had that effect. "But if you're not," he continued, "it has to be the drugs. What are you doing these days?"

"Oh, I do whatever I can get my hands on," I said, laughing. "Cocaine, meth. Sometimes I just raid the medicine cabinet and take handfuls of whatever I find."

I was about to dive in and tell them all about mugging and the man in the alley when there was a stifled gasp from behind me. I turned to see my mom standing in the doorway, her hand over her mouth.

"Mom, no." I held up the phone to prove my innocence. "It's Colin and Lisa. I'm just... it was a joke."

Mom's expression shifted uncertainly between horror and fury. Settling on horror, she bellowed, *"Jonathan! Come up here. Now!"*

I hung up the phone as my dad arrived at the doorway. He wore a flowered apron and clutched a wooden spoon that dripped spaghetti sauce on the carpet.

"What?" he said, looking around the room anxiously. "What happened?"

"Your s... son's turned to drugs!" Mom's words sounded like they were being choked out of her.

"I'm not doing drugs." I rolled my eyes. "We were joking around. That's all."

My father wasn't a small man and could have been a linebacker in another life. So the apron he wore looked more like a bib. He tapped the sauce-laden spoon on one hand, pursed his lips, and then ran his hand through his hair, oblivious to the fact that in doing so he left a streak of red across his head. "Drugs, Dean?"

This was getting ridiculous. I struggled to clamp down my anger. "We were just joking around. I told them about the whole hallucination thing and they were just trying to make me feel better."

"I think it was just a misunderstanding, hon." My dad stepped next to me and draped his arm over my shoulder and looked at my mom. "Kids joke about serious issues. It's normal." He turned to me. "If your friends offer you drugs—"

"They're not going to offer me drugs, Dad. You both know Colin and Lisa. You know they'd never do that." I turned to my mom and sighed. "But if they do, I'll say no."

She wasn't looking at me anymore. Instead her brows were furrowed. She was focused on my dad's head. "What's in your hair?"

"My what?" He lifted his hand toward his head and paused when he saw his sauce-smeared palm. As if on cue, the smoke detector from the kitchen started beeping. *"My sauce!"* He charged past my mom and back down the stairs.

My mom ignored the ruckus coming from the kitchen and moved forward to hug me. She held me at arm's length. "You know better, right?"

I nodded.

She wiped her face with her sleeve. "I'd better go make sure your father doesn't burn the place down."

I plopped myself on my bed and thought about Mrs. Farnsworthy again. *If this keeps up, I might need drugs after all.*

CHAPTER 8

At 1:38 AM, it happened again. This time I was half asleep, or maybe I was completely asleep. I can't be sure. What I am sure about is that Mr. Utlet was suddenly kneeling beside my bed. The emerald glow of my alarm clock illuminated his face. I shot up, flattened myself against the wall at the edge of my bed, and watched as my neighbor emptied the air in his lungs with a shriek that seemed to shake the entire room. In a blink, it was over, and I was alone, trembling at the corner of the mattress.

Whatever was wrong with me, it was getting worse. And I wasn't sure how much more I could take.

Morning was like a kick in the shins: unexpected and painful.

The few brief moments of sleep I had managed to steal were filled with images of screaming neighbors, horrifying teachers, and ape-like thieves. My body ached from being so tense all night. Even my jaw hurt. I showered, then dragged myself downstairs and paused just outside the kitchen. *It's my birthday*, I remembered. If I knew my mom, she'd have some kind of grand affair waiting for me: balloons, streamers, and perhaps some kind of huge breakfast. The only thing I knew: I couldn't tell my dad about the other hallucinations. I'd be psycho-analyzed for the next three years. Instead, I took a deep breath, forced a smile, and rounded the corner.

Becky was alone at the table, attacking a towering stack of pancakes as if she only had minutes to eat them all. She looked up and gave me a frizzy-haired sneer.

"Where're Mom and Dad?" I asked.

"Out," she mumbled through a mouthful of food.

I looked at the pancakes and suddenly felt famished. "Are there any... um... "

"Nope."

"Well, do you think I could have a couple of yours?"

Becky groaned, stabbed one of the pancakes with her fork, moved it to an empty plate, and shoved the plate toward me.

"Wow, thanks." It was entirely out of character for Becky to do something nice, and I considered for just a moment that she might have poisoned the pancake. But it had been on her plate, so I decided it was safe, and I started eating before she could change her mind and demand it back.

"I guess since it's your birthday, I'll share. Well, that, and because you're a *hero*."

"*Hero?* What are you talking about?"

She gave the newspaper on the table a shove and it skidded toward me.

The Abbotsford Gazette wasn't the city's main source of news, but it was delivered to everyone for free. There, smack in the middle of the front page, was a picture of my battered face. I remembered the reporter snapping a photo the previous morning. The headline read: "Local Boy Stops Attack." The article used the word "hero" more than once, and by the time I reached the end of the story, a big weight had lifted off me. I'd had a pit in my stomach about going back to school. I knew most people thought my outburst in Mrs. Farnsworthy's class had been a prank, but I was afraid it was only a matter of time before I blew my cover by having another hallucination. And here was the perfect attention shifter—and on my birthday no less. Obviously, attention would not shift *from* me, but at least it would shift to something more positive. I was no hero, but I would take what I could get.

"You look pleased," Becky said, her tone all sarcasm. "Hoping people will forget about your little screaming fit yesterday?"

Becky was in seventh grade and in a different school, so the fact that she knew anything about my... episode... stunned me. "How did you... ?"

She waved a dismissive hand. "Jasmine, of course."

Jasmine was Colin's sister and every bit as annoying as Becky. I'd be talking to Colin about keeping his mouth shut around his sister when I next saw him.

Becky forked another chunk of pancake into her mouth. "Apparently, Colin thinks you're *possessed*." She nodded toward the newspaper. "I told her you're just a big wimp, but now I think maybe you *are* possessed. It's not like you to be brave."

"Gee, thanks," I said.

A car door slammed in the driveway and Becky jumped to her feet. She grabbed my plate, tipped the last couple of pancakes from her plate to mine, and shoved it back at me. She was at the kitchen sink looking very pleased when my parents walked through the backdoor, each carrying a pile of newspapers.

"Oh, you're up," my mom said. She put her stack on the counter and walked over to give me a hug. "And I see you're well into your birthday breakfast."

"*My* birthday breakfast?"

"See, Jonathan," she added, looking toward my dad. "And you thought Becky might try to eat it."

I glared across the kitchen at my sister. "But she—"

"How many of those papers can you possibly need?" Becky interrupted as a crooked smile inched across her lips. When it came to sibling rivalry, my sister was no slouch. I vowed revenge.

My dad held up a copy of the *Gazette*. "You read the article, right, champ?"

"Um... yeah, Dad. I read it."

"You saved that man's life, Dean," he said. "I wouldn't be surprised if you get a medal."

"Whoa, whoa," I said. "Just slow down. I didn't save anyone. In fact, the article says the man's still in the hospital. And just so there's no confusion, all I did was call 911. No, I didn't even do that, I just held my wallet to my ear. That's it." My mom made a gesture like she wanted to speak, but I cut her off. "Thank you for the breakfast, Mom. It was delicious. But please, when my friends come here tonight, don't make a big deal of this whole hero nonsense." I knew Colin would probably already make a big enough deal of the whole thing on his own. He didn't need help.

I grabbed my jacket from the back of the chair and made for the door, pausing to add, "And don't make a big deal about my birthday either, okay?"

My dad laughed. "Modesty. I like that."

"Me too," my mom said. "I'll pick you and your friends up after school."

"No, it's okay. I think we'll walk, or we might take the bus into town."

"You'll call when you decide, right?"

"Jeez, Mom. Yes, I'll call."

I looked across the kitchen. Becky pointed at me and started rocking an imaginary baby in her arms as she mouthed the word "pathetic."

"Nice hair, Becky," I called as I reached for the door. I heard a loud growl and the stomping of feet before the door shut behind me. *This could shape up to be a good day*, I thought.

Boy, was I wrong.

CHAPTER 9

Colin and Lisa were waiting at my locker when I got to school.

"What's the deal?" Colin held up a cut-out of the article from the *Gazette*'s front page. "You never told us this was the reason you were late on Friday."

"Yeah, Dean. Why didn't you say something?" Lisa added.

"I was a bit preoccupied, what with all the hallucinations."

"Yeah, but now your hallucinations make sense," Lisa said.

"They do?" Colin looked confused, and I was pretty sure my expression matched his exactly.

"Stress," she said. "Stress can make people see things. You had to fight off a couple of murderous thugs. I'd say that qualifies as stressful."

"I fought off murderous thugs?" I looked at Colin and then back to Lisa. "Where did you get the idea that I fought anyone? It doesn't even say that in the paper."

"It says you stopped them," Lisa said. "And your

face was all bruised up, so I figured you must've—"

Before Lisa could finish, Eric Feldman's nasally voice came from behind me. "Well, if it isn't our resident hero."

I spun around, sick of Eric's teasing and ready to face the little twerp. But as soon as I saw Rodney, I recoiled. Perhaps because Eric's oversized goon was wearing all black and seemed really pale, or perhaps because he'd always looked a bit zombie-like but I'd never really noticed before... for whatever reason, I thought I was having another hallucination. My heart hammering, I turned slowly to my friends. "Do you see him?" My voice was a whisper.

Lisa stepped beside me and placed her hand on my arm. Colin cringed visibly as he mouthed, "Dude."

"Of course they see him, you wacko." Eric gave Rodney a jab. "I told you he was nuts."

Rodney always looked a bit puzzled. I was pretty sure he was so angry because he was confused all the time. But as he scratched the side of his stubbly face and glared down at me, he looked even more puzzled than usual. I wondered if I looked confused too, or just scared. It was tough to decide which feeling I should focus on.

"C'mon, Rodney," Eric said. "We have shop class. Besides, if you keep looking at Dean, I think he might just wet himself."

Rodney laughed and lunged at Colin just enough to make him flinch. Then Rodney slouched his way down the hall after Eric.

"Are you okay?" Lisa asked.

"Yeah, dude," Colin said as he watched Rodney round the corner. "What's going on?"

"Something's happening to me," I muttered.

"What do you mean?" Lisa asked.

I stood up and pulled my friends into an alcove at the end of the block of lockers. "Last Friday," I began, "I was running late… "

I told them everything: what happened in the alley, the first two hallucinations, Mrs. Farnsworthy, and even Mr. Utlet.

"*Glimpse?*" Lisa asked. "That's what the guy who got attacked said to you? Just *glimpse*, and that's it?"

"In the attackee's defense," Colin said, smirking, "he had just gotten his butt kicked. I can see why he might not have been too chatty."

"You think this is funny?" I asked. My hands were shaking, from fear mostly but from anger too. "I'm seeing things." My voice lowered to a whisper. "I'm hallucinating some scary stuff. It looks real. Like they're… "

Colin and Lisa inched forward. "Like they're what?" Lisa prodded.

My voice dropped to a whisper. "Like these people were dying. Or maybe they are already dead and I am seeing their ghosts... which I know doesn't make much sense considering I saw Mrs. F and Mr. Utlet, and they're alive. I... I don't know how to explain it, but something's wrong with me. I'm barely keeping it together."

Colin looked down at the floor and twisted his foot as if grinding a bug into the tile. "Sorry. You're right. Your hallucinations are not funny." Then he looked at me. "So you help this guy, and then you start hallucinating? Do you think he did something to you?"

"Besides splattering blood all over my shirt?"

"Gross," Lisa said.

"Yeah, that is sorta gross," Colin said. "But I mean, are you sure he didn't mutter something else besides *glimpse*? A chant, perhaps?"

Lisa and I looked at each other, then turned back to Colin and asked at the same time, "A chant?"

Colin looked determined. "Yeah, in the movies it's always a bunch of Latin that ends with the word *mortis*." He leaned forward. "Did he say *mortis*?"

I turned to Lisa, who looked at least as confused as I felt, then back to Colin. "What the heck are you talking about?"

He threw up his hands. "A curse, obviously!"

"You think I'm cursed?"

"Don't you? I mean, if you were seeing people who were actually dead, I might think you had some kind of superpower, like maybe you could communicate with them or, better yet, command them to do stuff for you. They could even spy on people for you." He smiled and sighed disappointedly. "But since you're just having messed up hallucinations about living people, it's a lot less cool and seems more like a curse."

Lisa turned to me. "Didn't I tell you he watches too many movies?"

"I think I said that too," I added dryly.

"I don't watch that many movies," Colin defended. "It's not possible to watch *too many* movies."

"Your mind just shoots straight to the most impossible explanation on its own?" Lisa asked. "You don't even consider things that actually make sense?" She crossed her arms over her chest. "And, yeah, you can watch too many movies. You have a bigger movie library than Netflix."

That was true. Colin did have a lot of movies, but you couldn't really blame him. His dad was a location scout for a movie production company, and his mom used to be an actress. So movies sort of ran in his family.

"He said *glimpse*," I said. "That's it. I don't think

that sounds much like a curse."

Colin tapped his chin thoughtfully.

Lisa sighed. "Dean, don't listen to him. It's just stress—that's what makes the most sense. Your hallucinations started after you saw two men beating another man in the alley and then you got trampled at an electronics store. One of those things would have been enough to freak anyone out, Dean. Especially the beating. It freaked you out, right?"

"I guess so."

"Dean, don't—" The morning bell cut her off. "We'll talk later, at lunch or on the way to your birthday party after school."

"Oh, man, I'm sorry." Colin put his hand on my shoulder. "Happy birthday."

"Yeah, thanks," I said. "Maybe if I make a wish right now instead of waiting until I blow out the candles, the rest of my birthday will be insanity-free."

"It's worth a try," he said.

I forced a smile and headed to class. As I walked down the hallway, I closed my eyes for a brief second and muttered a single wish. *I just want everything to make sense.* I guess in the end I got what I wished for.

Mr. Woodward—or *Woody*, as he preferred to be called—was an ex-army sergeant who had served two tours of duty in Vietnam. He was also my English teacher. He had a slight limp, the result of a landmine incident that left his right side partially paralyzed. Still, he managed to stand ramrod straight and only hunched the slightest bit when he walked. Everything he said sounded like marching orders, and even though it might not have been true, it was widely believed that if you spoke out of turn in Woody's class, you'd wake up strapped to a metal bed frame with a couple car batteries wired to your nipples. With a rumor like that, you don't risk standing out. No matter who you are.

"Curse!" Woody barked when I entered the class.

"Yes, sir?"

"I understand you killed a couple muggers last Friday."

The class gasped in unified shock and spun in their chairs to look at me.

"W... what? No, sir, I didn't kill any—"

"No matter, son. They probably deserved it." He placed one hand on his desk and leaned forward. "What did you use? A knife? A rock?" He looked down and flexed his fingers. "Or just your bare hands?"

"Sir, I wasn't even the one who called the—"

He held up his hand. "No, no. Better not say anything

else. Let it die down a bit." A smile threatened the corners of his mouth. "Don't want you saying anything that might be used against you, right?" He gave a curt nod. "Let's get started."

I took my seat, a bit confused—which wasn't that odd in Woody's class—and cracked open my copy of *Macbeth*. Now, Shakespeare is tough enough to follow as it is. So if you ever find yourself having to listen to it read in the monotonous chant of a former military man, just forget about it.

Woody limped toward his desk. "*Macbeth* is William Shakespeare's shortest tragedy."

The large desk in front of the room groaned as Woody sat on the front corner of it. "Act one, scene one: the play opens amidst thunder and lightning."

Boom!

The class reacted with a unified start and all eyes shot to our teacher, whose gaze was now fixated on the door. *What was that?* I felt the building shake and wondered if Mr. Woodward had timed a special effect to wake up the class. Then the fire alarm sounded and people—both inside and outside the classroom—started screaming.

"*Hey!*" Woody shouted.

The screams in the classroom quieted, but I could still hear others in the hall.

"We don't panic. We've done this before. It's just like the drills." He moved to the exit doors. "We walk quickly and quietly out the west exit." His coal black eyes scanned the room. "Understand?"

The class began to move down the hall toward the exit. Students filed out from other classrooms and shuffled down the corridor while teachers barked orders. Everyone seemed to suck in a collective breath as smoke started to chase us like a rippling black snake.

I glanced over my shoulder as I followed Woody and my classmates. A black cloud billowed from the far end of the hall. Where was Lisa? And Colin? I tried to remember their schedules. What class did they have this period?

The black cloud moved closer. I turned back to Woody. He was at the exit, holding the door open and urging everyone to hurry. I started running just as a second explosion boomed through the hallway.

CHAPTER 10

Black smoke billowed from the east wing of the school. The bits of broken glass that had managed to stay in the window frames reflected back the amber lights of emergency vehicles. Students scattered around the parking lot like startled birds.

"Biology lab." I recognized Lisa's voice from somewhere behind me and spun around. Tiny pieces of debris clung to her hair, which was now gray rather than the usual deep brown. Soot coated her face, smearing around her eyes and cheeks as though she had been crying.

"Jeez, Lisa, are you okay?"

"I'm not hurt. It was the biology lab."

"Where were you?"

"History. Whatever happened blew a hole in the wall to our class."

"Was anyone hurt?"

Lisa's lip quivered, and she looked as if she wanted to say something but wasn't sure how to form the words. My stomach twisted. I suddenly had a sinking feeling that what she wasn't telling me involved Colin.

I looked past her, over the groups of people huddled nearby. "Where's Colin?"

"Colin's fine," Lisa said. "He's looking for you too. We both were."

My pulse slowed. "Thank God. But if you knew it was the biology lab, why'd you worry? You know my schedule. I had English."

She blinked and turned to the crowd.

What isn't she telling me?

"Colin!" she raised her hand. "Over here."

Colin weaved through the crowd. When he made it over to us, he looked back and forth between Lisa and me like he was waiting for me to react to a joke that I hadn't yet heard. "Well? Did you tell him?"

"Tell me what?" I asked.

"I didn't tell him yet," Lisa said. "I wanted to wait for you."

"Tell me what?"

"About Mrs. Farnsworthy."

"What about her?"

Colin looked at Lisa, then back to me. "The explosion, Dean. She was right in the middle of it."

"W... what?" My earlier hallucination of her screaming face flashed in my mind. No way. It couldn't be related.

"Look, we don't know anything," Lisa said. "But

she was just standing there, and then the wall behind her exploded. I saw her getting taken away by the ambulance. It didn't look good."

"What the heck happened?" I asked.

Lisa shook her head. "All I know is that the biology lab exploded. And a bunch of people are hurt. Loads of people have been taken to the hospital on stretchers. But the paramedics were doing CPR on Mrs. Farnsworthy. I saw it." She looked at me as if I had the answer to some riddle scribbled on my forehead.

"What?" I asked. "Why are you looking at me like that?"

"When did you have your vision?"

"Vision? You mean my hallucination?"

"Start of first period," Colin said. "Maybe ten minutes in."

I blinked. What was she getting at? I opened my mouth. "Are you saying that—"

"I'm not saying anything. Yet. But I think it's pretty clear what we have to do," she said.

"Is it?" Colin asked.

"We go to the hospital." She looked back at the school. "Dean, you said yourself that you saw Mrs. Farnsworthy, right? I think we need to go see her."

"You think Mrs. Farnsworthy has something to do with my hallucinations?"

"She was your hallucination, Dean."

Colin nodded. "She's got a point. I say we go."

We each called our parents and told them not to worry. It took the better part of twenty minutes to convince my mom that we were fine, and by the time she let me hang up, we were already on the bus, halfway to the hospital.

"What do we do if she's not okay?" I looked at Colin, then Lisa. "What would that mean?"

Lisa shrugged and then cleared her throat. "Isn't that guy from the alley in the hospital too?"

Colin sprang up from the seat. "We should go see him."

I turned to Lisa. "Don't tell me you're buying into Colin's curse theory now." She shrugged and I added, "The last thing that man needs are visitors."

"It's not all that far-fetched," Colin said. "You save him, he mutters some cryptic word at you, and all of a sudden you go nuts."

"He's not nuts," Lisa said.

Colin drew a breath. "Well, he's nuts or... " He chewed his lip for a second. "You have some kind of psychic ability." His eyes widened. "I've heard of people becoming psychic after getting into an accident."

Lisa wiped a sleeve across her face and turned to me. "I'm not saying I believe Colin. I still think your hallucinations have to do with stress. But it might help for you to see that he's okay, and that Mrs. Farnsworthy is—" Her voice cracked.

"She'll be okay," Colin said. "She's ex-KGB, remember? It's going to take more than a little explosion to hurt her."

Lisa looked at her shoes. "You didn't see her."

Colin opened his mouth then closed it. He cocked his head as if he wanted me to say something to make Lisa feel better. "Fine. We'll go see him," I said.

Lisa looked up.

"Good," Colin said, relieved. "It's settled then."

"Do we even know what we're going to say to him?" I asked.

"Yeah," Colin said. "We're going to ask him what kind of voodoo spell he cast to make you see... " He trailed off and glanced out the window. "What is it you're seeing anyway? Visions? Aberrations?"

"Apparitions," Lisa said.

"What?"

"You mean apparitions, not aberrations."

Colin shrugged and turned back to me. "I mean ghosts, the otherworldly, the—"

"I get it," I said.

"Look, guys," Lisa said, "let's just take this one step at a time, okay? First, we check on Mrs. Farnsworthy. Then we find the guy from the alley, and we talk to him. Let's not jump to conclusions here. Dean's been going through a lot: the stress of final exams, the stress of witnessing a crime... " Her eyes glossed as her voice trailed off. She turned her head and wiped her eyes again, leaving fresh smudges on her face.

Though she had mentioned it before, it only just hit me that Lisa had witnessed the explosion firsthand. Seeing something like that would have to be difficult to come back from. I wanted to reassure her that things would be okay, but the words just wouldn't come. After the past few days, I wasn't sure things would be okay.

Luckily, Colin picked up the slack. "Everything's going to be fine," he said unconvincingly. "Don't worry, we'll help Dean sort out... " He and Lisa both glanced at me for a fraction of a second before looking away.

Great. Now my friends couldn't even talk or look at me without wondering if I was a freak. "It could all be just some bizarre coincidence," I offered.

"It has to be," Lisa said, mostly under her breath.

CHAPTER 11

The hospital was at a level of chaos I couldn't have imagined. Ambulances lined up one behind the other, waiting their turn to drop off an injured student, only to leave with their sirens on, no doubt going back to the school. Inside was even worse. Droves of parents clogged the nurses' station, desperate to know the condition of their children.

"We're never going to get any information there," Lisa said, pointing to the crowd.

Colin placed his hands on our backs and pushed us forward, through the crowd and toward the elevator. "We don't need to wait," he said. He punched the UP button. "There's a nurses' station on every floor. And each floor can tell you what you need to know."

Colin certainly wasn't the sharpest kid you'd meet, but if he said something about hospitals, I believed him. He had broken more bones than anyone I knew, and over the years, I'd visited him dozens of times. Usually he ended up in the hospital after doing something stupid — last time he'd broken a couple ribs falling out of a tree while chasing a squirrel. The time before that, he thought it would be cool to try riding his skateboard while wearing roller blades.

We stepped off the elevator at the second floor and squinted against the harsh lights reflecting off the polished linoleum. The area seemed utterly deserted compared to the floor below. Colin wasted no time and walked straight to the nurses' station. "Excuse me, ma'am."

A middle-aged nurse stood up from behind her counter. She had short, boy-cut hair and wore purple scrubs. She peered down at the three of us. Concern flashed across her face when she saw Lisa's soot-covered face. "You kids must be coming from that school explosion. Are you okay?"

"We're fine, ma'am." Colin leaned against the counter. "We're just trying to find out if our teacher is okay. Her name's Mrs. Farnsworthy. We would've asked downstairs, but it's just crazy down there."

The nurse nodded. "I've been down there." She looked off to the left and sighed. "Those poor parents must be terrified." She turned to her computer and tapped a few keys. "That's nice of you kids to come see how your teacher is doing." She tapped a few more keys. "Mrs. Farnsworthy, you say?"

Colin nodded.

A moment passed while the nurse read whatever was on her screen. "I'm sorry, there's nothing in my computer yet—they're busy down there; it might not have been entered yet. Don't you worry, though, I'll bet your teacher will be fine."

She smiled, and then when she looked at me, her eyes widened.

"Wait. You're that boy." She shuffled some papers on the desk and held up a copy of the *Abbotsford Gazette*. "That's you, isn't it?"

"That's him, ma'am," Colin said. "Our local hero."

"That was just the bravest thing I had ever heard of, young man." She leaned over the counter. "Is it true you fought them off all by yourself?"

"He did, ma'am," Colin said, slapping my back. "Dean's the bravest kid I know. He took on a group of murderous thieves just to help his fellow man. Can you imagine the courage?"

I rolled my eyes. "It really wasn't like—"

"That's the other reason we're here," Lisa said, squaring her shoulders. "We'd really like to see the man Dean saved. You know, just to make sure he's okay."

The nurse's lips thinned into a grim line. "Mr. Vidmar is down the hall. But I'm sorry to say that it doesn't look good. He's in really rough shape."

Vidmar, I thought. The name sounded foreign. "Is

his family here?"

She shook her head. "He has a brother. The admitting doctor spoke to him when we finally tracked him down. I know he's on his way, but he might not get here until tomorrow.

"Do you think we could see him anyway?" Lisa prodded. "We came a very long way."

The nurse smiled. "I don't see the harm, but you'll need to make it quick. The doctors will be making their rounds soon. Besides, some visitors might do the poor man some good." She gestured down the hall. "He's in Room 245, but he might not be awake."

"We'll just look in on him then," Lisa said. "Thank you."

Room 245 was at the end of the curved hallway, and outside his room was a metal trolley covered in binders. "Vidmar" was written on one of the binder spines, and all three of us stopped when we saw it.

"You think it will say if he's going to make it?" Colin asked.

"You can't read that," Lisa said. "It's private."

"Please. Don't you think there might be something useful in there?" Colin reached over and pulled the binder from the stack and opened it up. Lisa and I leaned over Colin's shoulder and glanced down at the page.

Notes scrawled in black ink covered the whole page.

There were also a series of dates with notations beside them. Some of the writing was hard to read, but several key words jumped out. *Electrocution, multiple beatings/ muggings, mentally unstable, delusional, committed to psychiatric facility.* I scanned over the rest of the page and stopped at a note at the bottom: *"Brother reports several suicide attempts, the latest being January 2008—patient jumped from a bridge."*

"That's enough," Lisa said, reaching out and closing the binder. "We shouldn't read that stuff. It's not right. Let's just talk to him."

All of us were shocked by the things we had read. The chart was nearly an inch thick. We hadn't really expected the man I saved to be—I searched for the word—unstable. Now the fact that Mr. Vidmar was still even alive defied logic. "You're right, Lisa. Let's go."

The three of us entered the room and stopped by the door. "Rough" didn't begin to describe the shape of the man. Purple, orange, and brown bruises, along with at least a dozen lacerations, covered his face. Dark hair poked out from below a white gauze that formed a thick band around his head, and his arms, from wrists to armpits, were set in white casts. Machines running wires to his chest *beeped* and *hummed* out various rhythms that let us know he was at least alive. I guessed that he was in his mid to early thirties, though with all the bandages, it was difficult to tell.

Lisa peeked in a small backpack next to his bed. I recognized it from the alley.

"Stopwatches," she said.

"What?" I asked.

"This bag." She reached in and pulled out a handful of stopwatches. "There's got to be a dozen of them here. She flipped one over in her hand and examined the back. Then she grabbed another and examined the back of it. "They all have initials on the back. R.T., G.H., D.C., S.W.—"

"Dean Curse," Colin interrupted.

I looked at him, confused.

"D.C." He pointed over the bed to Lisa. "She said one of the initials was D.C., like Dean Curse. Maybe he was going to give it to you for your birthday."

"Don't be an idiot, Colin," Lisa said as she stuffed the watches back into the bag. "They could mean anything."

Colin shrugged. "I wasn't being serious."

"He's asleep," I said. "We should go. Maybe come back tomorrow."

Lisa plucked up a newspaper from a table beside the bed. "Looks like he was reading your article." She turned to put the paper back on the table and inadvertently knocked a cup of orange juice over Colin's shoes.

"Oops." She tossed the newspaper to the foot of Mr. Vidmar's bed and reached for the stack of paper towels on a nearby shelf.

"That better be orange juice and not a urine sample," Colin said, grimacing at his feet.

The copy of the *Gazette* had landed partially open, and as I turned to pick it up, I froze. There was an article on page two that caught my attention. I could only see half of it, but what I saw was enough. With shaking hands, I reached out and opened the paper completely.

"What is it, Dean?" Colin was by my side in a flash.

I pointed to the article.

Colin read the title aloud. "Pile-Up on Highway 1 Claims Three Lives."

"That's awful," Lisa said.

"It's n... not the article," I choked. Beneath the headline were the pictures of the three victims. The woman I'd seen screaming in the foyer and the overweight man who had freaked me out in the kitchen were among them. Seeing the photos made my stomach drop—the man and woman looked so happy and normal—not at all the way I had seen them in my hallucinations.

My mind struggled to make sense of it all. I didn't recognize the faces from anywhere other than my crazy visions. "Those are the two people I saw first."

"What? Who?" Colin asked.

I tapped the two pictures.

"Are you sure?"

"Yes. Completely. I'd never forget those faces."

"They're dead," Lisa stated the obvious. "You're seeing hallucinations of people who are... dead. Or going to die." Her voice lowered to a whisper. "Is that even possible?"

Collin grabbed the paper and flipped through it until he found the page he was looking for. He slapped it down. "Did you see any of these people?"

He had opened the page to the Obituaries section. A dozen or so people who had died over the last few days stared back at me from their photographs.

"No. None of them."

"What about the first people you saw?" Collin added. "Do you recognize them? Know them from anywhere?"

"No."

Colin turned back to the article about the accident and gave it a quick read. "You're definitely sure you've never met these people?"

"Yeah, I'm sure, Colin. I've never met them."

"Maybe just in passing, Dean," Lisa urged. "Think about it."

"I'm telling you. I've never seen them before. Not recently, that's for sure. After the mugging, I went straight home... no, wait! Gadget Emporium!"

"What?" Colin asked.

"I stopped at Gadget Emporium. Remember? I told you, that's where all my bruises came from. It was the grand opening. There were hundreds of people there. I was trampled by at least half of them. They could've been there."

Lisa chewed her lip for a second and then said, "What if these hallucinations are really... visions?"

"*Dean*."

All three of us jumped and looked down at the newspaper. For a second I think we all thought that one of the faces in the newspaper had said my name, and it wasn't until we heard it again that we realized it was coming from the top of the bed.

"Mr. V... Vidmar?"

The man's swollen eyes fluttered, then opened and searched around the room. He coughed and pointed at me. "Dean Curse?"

"Y... yes, sir."

His eyes drooped and opened again. He seemed to be struggling to stay awake. "You c... came. I kn... knew you vud." He struggled to speak, and I had to really concentrate to understand him through his thick Russian accent.

I stepped closer to the bed, and the man strained to shift his weight.

"Sir, we just wanted to come—"

"I'm s... sorry," the man rasped.

"Sorry?" I said. I wondered if we should call a doctor or nurse—he sounded almost out of breath.

He glanced at my friends and then back to me. "I'm sorry, Dean. I h... had to give it t... to someone. I th... thought I was dying. I couldn't let it die with me."

"You're going to be fine," I said. "Just hang in—"

"You had to give him what?" Colin interrupted. "What couldn't die with you?"

"Dmitri... ask Dmitri about Pripyat."

"Preewhat?" I asked. "Who?"

The machines at his bedside started beeping faster until they sounded like a group of panicking robots.

"What'd you have to give to Dean?" Colin pressed.

"Colin," Lisa scolded. "Stop. We need to call a nurse."

"What are these kids doing in here?"

I spun around as three people—a woman in a white knee-length lab coat who I figured was a doctor and a man and woman in faded blue scrubs—strode into the room. "We were just—"

"Are you family?" the doctor asked.

"N... no."

"Nurse! Get these kids out of here."

A different nurse than the one we'd met rushed into

the room and placed her hands on Colin's shoulders. "C'mon, you three. You can visit again tomorrow. He needs his rest."

"Wait," Colin demanded, "we still have questions."

"Check his oh-two stats," one of the doctors said.

The man in scrubs went to the head of the bed and pressed his stethoscope to Mr. Vidmar's chest. "Sir," she said, "I just need you to relax and take a couple deep breaths."

Mr. Vidmar barked something in Russian and then craned his neck around the doctor. "Save them, Dean," he said, his voice stern and even. "Save as many as you can."

The doctor pressed Mr. Vidmar back into the bed. "I need you to lay down, sir."

I wanted to ask more questions, but the nurse grabbed my wrist and pulled me out of the room. "You three certainly managed to get Mr. Vidmar excited," she said. "But you heard the doctor—he needs his rest. I'm afraid that at least for the time being, Mr. Vidmar will only be able to have visits from family. Perhaps in a few weeks you could try again." She rushed back into the room and swung the door behind her. It latched shut in our faces with a heavy *click*.

CHAPTER 12

We lingered outside Mr. Vidmar's room for a few minutes, hoping the doctors would come out and tell us we could see him again. They didn't.

"Well, that was a big waste of time," Colin said, pacing the width of the hall. "We didn't get any of the answers we wanted to get."

"That was awful," Lisa muttered. "That poor man."

Colin looked at me. "Who's Dmitri?"

I shook my head and turned away. All I could think about were Mr. Vidmar's words.

"What did he mean when he said '*Save them all*'? Do you think he was telling you to save Mrs. Farnsworthy?" Lisa asked.

"I was thinking the same thing," Colin said.

"Why?" I said. "What could I possibly do? She's here now. Doctors are treating her."

Colin stopped pacing and shook his finger at me. "What did he mean he had to give it to you and that he couldn't let it die with him?" He paused for a second and then said, "I still think it could be a curse."

Lisa shook her head. "Are you still on that? Curses don't exist, and even if they did, why would he curse Dean? Dean saved him. You don't curse heroes."

"So maybe it's not a curse and it's something that seems like a curse," Colin defended. "Maybe it *is* some kind of superpower but Dean just doesn't know how to control it."

"If feels more like a curse," I said.

"It's not a curse," Lisa said.

Colin muttered, "It's *like* a curse."

Lisa pointed at Mr. Vidmar's door. "Well, he's the only one who can tell us what's going on. Let's not jump to conclusions until we actually speak to him. Maybe when things calm down a bit the nurses will change their minds and let us see him again—at least for long enough to find out who this Dmitri guy is." She peered through the small window in the door leading to Mr. Vidmar's room. "Poor man."

I suddenly wanted to be anywhere but here. Everything was just getting to be too much. "We should go."

"You don't think we should wait around?" Lisa looked through the window again. "Make sure Mr. Vidmar's okay?"

I turned and headed toward the elevator. "I can't. You two stay. I need some fresh air. I'll be back." But by the time I reached the elevator, Lisa was next to me, and Colin came running in just as the doors were about to close.

"We should stick together," Colin said. "If you see anything else, we should be nearby."

"Besides," Lisa added, "I could use some fresh air too. This is all a bit... overwhelming."

The main entrance was still flooded with distraught family members and media people who couldn't fit in the emergency room. A woman wearing a Global TV windbreaker stepped into our path and pointed a microphone at my chest. "Hey, I recognize you. You're that kid who played hero the other day." A bright light shone in my face. My fight-or-flight reflex kicked in, and I chose flight. I dodged to the left, ducked around a couple of other people, and pushed through the front door. Lisa was only a few paces behind me, but Colin was nowhere to be seen. I didn't stop, even though my heart was railing against my ribs and my stomach was ready to hurl out my breakfast. I ran past the news vans and made it halfway through the long-term parking lot before I stopped.

I laced my fingers behind my head and looked up at the sky. I could hear Lisa huffing for breath beside me. I turned back to the hospital and saw Colin walking calmly out of the main doors. He started jogging in our direction when he saw us.

"It's going to be okay," Lisa said to me. "We're all a

bit freaked out right now."

"Oh, really?" I snapped. "You're freaked out? Are you hallucinating people screaming like they are going to die, only to find out that they actually *are* about to die?"

"Dean, we don't know that they're... that they're all dead," Lisa said.

"A... actually we... do," Colin huffed.

Lisa and I both turned.

"Well?" Lisa snapped, sounding as anxious as I felt.

"R... right, sorry." He stood up and heaved a couple big breaths. "That news chick, she wanted to know if we'd been at the school during the blast. I told her we had, and then she wanted to know how I felt about the accident and about... Mrs. Farnsworthy's death."

I blanched. "She's dead?"

"That's only half of it, Dean."

I looked up at Colin. "Half?"

"I saw Scott from my English class in there. He told me he heard that Mrs. F died in the ambulance."

"She did?" Lisa paled.

Lisa and Colin looked at each other as if they knew something I didn't. "So what?" I said. "What difference does that make?"

"If Mrs. F died in the ambulance," Colin said, "that means she died just a few minutes after the start of first period. And you had the first two hallucinations—" He stopped and shook his head. "No, not hallucinations—visions. You had your first two on Friday, but the paper said the crash happened on Saturday."

"Spit it out, Colin," I blurted. "What are you getting at?"

"Your visions," Colin said. "Your visions happened twenty-four hours before each death." He tapped his watch again. "I bet it was exactly twenty-four hours."

"That's ridiculous." Even as the words left my lips, I knew it wasn't. How could anything be ridiculous anymore? People I thought I had hallucinated were dead.

"Maybe," Colin said. "But maybe not." He paused for a second before adding, "Oh, and people were saying that there's no school tomorrow—maybe not for a few days." He smiled weakly, as though he hoped this good news would somehow offset the bad.

"We need to go." Lisa's voice was filled with fear.

"I thought you wanted to stay," I said, fighting to keep my voice from shaking. "See how Mr. Vidmar makes out?"

"We don't have time. We need to get to your house now."

"It's not even one o'clock yet," Colin said. "Dean told his mom we wouldn't be home until dinner."

"I'm not worried about that." Lisa looked at me as though there were something obvious I was missing.

Colin's eyes widened. "Your neighbor!"

I had hoped that the vision of Mr. Utlet screaming at my bedside had been a dream, but as I looked at Lisa's terrified expression, reality sank in and I considered the possibility that what I was seeing—these horrible images—were real. Mr. Vidmar's words suddenly made sense: "*Save them. Save as many as you can.*"

The bus stop was on the other side of the hospital, and we didn't stop running until we got there. On the bus, we claimed the back bench and discussed all the ways we could protect Mr. Utlet. We decided we'd get to Mr. Utlet's house and make sure he couldn't go anywhere. His house was probably the safest place for him, and we could watch it from my room until everyone was asleep, then sneak out and make sure nothing bad happened during the night.

Four visions and three deaths, I thought. Mr. Utlet wasn't going to be the fourth. I couldn't let that happen. I just couldn't.

CHAPTER 13

Mr. Utlet had the nicest lawn on the block. I made money cutting lawns one summer, and Mr. Utlet had hired me to cut his. When I was done, the old man used a ruler to make sure the blades were the same length, and then when he realized they weren't, he made me go over the whole thing again. I never offered to cut his lawn again.

"Get off my lawn!" Mr. Utlet shouted as he stormed out the back of his house, pumping his fist in the air.

Colin had ducked around the front of the house so he could let the air out of the tires on the old man's Buick. Lisa and I were supposed to distract him. That part was easy: all we had to do was stand on his grass.

"Are you deaf, or what?" Mr. Utlet growled.

"Hi, Mr. Utlet," Lisa said. She flashed an oversized smile, and Mr. Utlet cringed in response. "We just wanted to stop by and see how you were feeling."

"How I'm what?"

"*Feeling*, sir. How are you feeling?"

Mr. Utlet was old, not stupid, and his eyes turned to slits as he looked back and forth between Lisa and me, obviously trying to figure out just what kind of angle we were working.

"I'm not buying any of those damn chocolates you kids are always peddling. If you need money, get a job."

"Oh no, sir," Lisa said. "We don't have any chocolates." She took a step closer. "So you're fine, then? No chest pain? No difficulty breathing? Nothing like that?"

"What?" he bellowed. He wagged a stern finger at Lisa. "Young lady, just what are you getting at here?"

The bushes behind us rustled as Colin stepped out and joined us.

"Oh no, you don't," he said. "Not another one." He strode forward, grabbed Colin with one hand and me with the other, and hauled the two of us through his yard and onto his driveway. "Now, get!" he said, giving us a shove. "And no more cutting across my grass. Got it?"

"Yes, sir," I said.

"Sorry, sir," Colin added. He was trying to look solemn, but it was obvious he was having a difficult time keeping the smile off his face.

"Thank you, Mr. Utlet," Lisa said, beaming. "Stay safe today, okay?"

He waved his arm around as if he were batting insects away from his head. "Get!"

We started walking back across the street, but

turned around when we heard Mr. Utlet cursing. He looked around the yard and then gave the flattened tire on his Buick a kick. We watched as he moved to the back of the car and opened the trunk.

"I was worried about that," I said. "He's going to try to change the tire. He'll probably drop the whole car on himself."

"You were supposed to flatten two tires," Lisa scolded. "No one has two spare tires; everyone has one. Why didn't you just stick to the plan?"

"Relax," Colin said. "It was taking too long, and someone could've seen me. The car was unlocked, so I took care of it."

As if on cue Mr. Utlet cursed again and slammed his trunk shut.

"I hid the jack," Colin added proudly.

Mr. Utlet stuffed his keys in his pants' pocket, pulled the zipper of his jacket up to his chin, and started walking down the sidewalk.

"Where's he going?" Colin said, taking a step forward. "He's not supposed to go anywhere."

"Mr. Utlet!" I yelled. I ran across the street and blocked the man's path. Lisa and Colin were right behind me.

"Whaddaya want?" he grumbled.

"Where are you going?"

"Someone flattened my tire," he said. "And stole my jack." He pointed a finger at each of us. "You three wouldn't know anything about that, would you?"

We shook our heads.

"Well, when I find the culprit... " He shook his fist again.

I risked a quick glance at Colin. His face had paled. I was willing to bet that Mr. Utlet could take out a gang of street thugs with a wet towel and a bowl of prunes.

"And so you're just going for a walk then?" Lisa asked. She crossed her hands behind her back and wriggled the toe of her shoe on the pavement, playing the part of innocence. Colin looked ready to gag.

Mr. Utlet glared at the three of us. "That's none of your business."

"We're only asking because it's dangerous," she said.

"Dangerous? I can handle walking to a store." As if to prove it, he cracked the knuckles on his left hand one by one.

"We'll go to the store for you," Lisa offered quickly. "We can pick up what you need. That way you don't have to walk."

"Listen, kids." He hunched forward and put his finger an inch away from Lisa's nose. "If I could march across France and make it through with all my limbs, I sure as heck can make it two blocks to the drugstore!"

"It's for Scouts, sir," I lied.

"Scouts?" Mr. Utlet raised an eyebrow.

"That's right, sir," Colin said. "We're trying to get a badge for helping old people do stuff."

"Old people do... *stuff*?" That last word came out through clenched teeth.

"Civic duty badge," Lisa said.

"You're a Scout too?" he asked. "They let girls be Scouts?"

Lisa put two fingers to her temple and saluted. "Yes, sir."

"It's three fingers, kid."

"Huh?"

"The salute. It's supposed to be three fingers." He shook his head. "Fine. If you three need to do something to get a stinking badge, go and pick up my order from Henderson's. I'll call and tell them."

"Thank you, sir," we chimed.

He grunted and turned back to his house, pausing for a second to give his tire another kick as he passed.

Colin turned to me as soon as Mr. Utlet was back in his house. "Scouts?"

"It was the only thing I could think of. Plus, I think my parents buy cookies from them every year."

"That's Girl Guides," Lisa said.

"Oh, right."

Colin laughed. "I love Girl Guide cookies."

"It was good thinking, anyway," Lisa said. "Now let's hurry up before he decides it's a good time to reshingle his roof."

Henderson's Drugstore was only two blocks away, so we were back in no time. Mr. Utlet grumbled a "Thank you" when we delivered his groceries, and then chased us off his porch when Colin asked if he needed any help blending his food for dinner.

"What if he just dies in his sleep?" Lisa asked when we made it back to my room.

"That would suck," Colin said. "It would be impossible for us to stop something like that." He looked at me. "What do you think?"

"What do I think of what?"

"Of how the old goat's gonna die. I thought you might have some kind of ESP about the whole thing now."

"*Old goat?*" Lisa cocked her head. "I have no idea how I became friends with someone as insensitive as you."

"I remember," Colin said, laughing. "You were getting pelted by snowballs and Dean and I rescued you."

Lisa rolled her eyes. "That's not how I remember it.

I think I was the one that came and rescued *you*."

Colin ignored her. "Well, my point is we know when the guy's *supposed* to die, so we *can* save him. We're going to be heroes."

"Or maybe we should just call 911," Lisa said.

"Now?" Colin pulled out his cell phone.

"No, not now," Lisa said. "Tonight. Dean said he saw Mr. Utlet at around one-thirty in the morning, so maybe we should just call around one."

"And say what?" I asked. "'There's a good chance that the old man next door is about to die?'"

Colin laughed. "I'd like to see the operator's face when we say that."

"We're *not* saying that." I paced the length of the room and then turned back to my friends. "Look, this is stupid. I thought it was a good idea, but now it's just plain stupid." Colin and Lisa opened their mouths to speak, but I cut them off. "I'm not some psychic. I don't see the future. I helped some crazy guy in the street and it stressed me out and I had a couple minor... episodes." I nodded toward Lisa. "Just like you said, it's stress. Except for the first two people, I'm only seeing people who freak me out."

"That old man freaks you out?" Colin said.

"He's like an ex-assassin or something," I mumbled. "He probably knows how to kill a guy with a toothpick."

"Dude, he probably doesn't even know his own name half the time. If he does die, it's gonna be because he choked on his prunes or something. "

"That's not how all old people are, Colin," Lisa chided. "Don't you have grandparents?"

"My grandpa calls me Charlie," Colin said. "Charlie was the name of his dog when he was a kid." He looked at Lisa, then at me. "Trust me, old people are nuts."

"You do kind of look like a dog named Charlie," Lisa muttered.

"Look," I said, "let's just keep to the plan and watch his house tonight. I'm sure it's going to turn out to be nothing. You'll see." I was surprised at how confident I sounded. Confidence that was completely at odds with the sinking feeling sweeping through me.

CHAPTER 14

Lisa, Colin, Becky, and my mom crowded around, staring at me with goofy smiles. They started singing as my dad made his way to the dining table carrying a chocolate cake alight with fourteen candles.

I winced. Thanks to Colin and Becky, my birthday song sounded a lot like a hyena getting fed through a wood chipper. I was grateful when it finally ended.

"Make a wish, champ," my dad said.

"Maybe you should wish not to be such a dork," Becky suggested.

Colin lifted his chin and puffed out his chest. "Just being friends with me means that Dean isn't a dork." He looked around the table. "That's just one of the benefits of my friendship."

Becky stared at him and then rolled her eyes. "Oh yeah, I can see that. Sure."

I closed my eyes, wished that nothing bad would happen tonight, and blew out the flames.

"B... birthday boy cuts the c... cake." I looked up at my mom. Tears were tracking their way down her cheeks.

Her hand shook as she handed me the knife. "My boy's so g... grown up," she sobbed.

"C'mon, Mom," Becky pleaded.

My dad put his arm around my mom and smiled. "It feels like just yesterday that we used to bathe Dean in the—"

"*Stop!*" Becky and I shouted together.

"Yeah, Mr. Curse," Colin added. "I don't like where that story is going, and I'm usually the one with the strong stomach."

I chopped up the cake, making sure to give Becky the smallest slice. She didn't seem to notice, as she was examining a jar with the number "46" written on the glass and a cockroach or a really large beetle or something lying on its back inside.

"What's the deal with your sister and those dead bugs?" Colin whispered.

I grimaced and shook my head. "You don't wanna know. Trust me."

"Before we eat," my dad said. "I want you kids to know that if you need to talk about what happened at your school, or about Mrs. Farnsworthy... " He cast his gaze around the table. "I'm here. You can talk to me. It's perfectly natural to have feelings you might not understand."

"Such a tragedy," my mom said. "That poor woman,

the grief her family must be going through right now. Unbearable. Plus the families of all those injured kids. I'm so glad none of you were injured."

I had never really thought about Mrs. Farnsworthy having a family. I always thought of her as someone who might have crawled out of a crypt somewhere or been hatched rather than born. But I suddenly remembered that she kept a framed photograph on her desk. It must have been a photo of her family: her kids and her husband. They'd be mourning her death. A knot of guilt twisted in my stomach—was it my fault that she had died?

"Okay, let's put those thoughts out of our heads for now." My dad reached up to his ear and pretended to pull something out and stuff it in his pocket. "But don't throw them away. It's important to deal with them." He paused and looked at us expectantly.

Colin glanced at me, clearly trying not to crack up. He reached up to his ear and put the invisible threads of his thoughts on the tabletop next to his plate. "I'll get to those after the cake," he said, making everyone laugh.

I spent the rest of the party trying to stop my parents from telling embarrassing stories about me. It felt good to relax. I even forgot to worry about Mr. Utlet. At least until Colin, Lisa, and I went up to my room. Then it was all we could talk about.

"So you still think we don't need to worry about your neighbor?" Lisa asked hesitantly.

I rubbed my hands on my jeans. "I *am* worried. I just don't like the idea that what I'm seeing could actually—"

"Be something real?" Colin finished.

"It can't be, right? I mean, I'm *not* psychic."

"Well, it's possible that it's nothing but a weird coincidence," Lisa said with a grimace, obviously unconvinced. "But just to be sure... "

"Okay," I said. "Let's stick to the plan we came up with on the bus. After everyone goes to sleep, we sneak out and watch his house. We keep the phone close. If we see anything... anything at all, we call 911."

"And if we don't see anything?" Lisa asked. "How will we explain that to the police?"

"There's a payphone at Henderson's," I said. "We can call the police from there at 1:15. That way, if they trace the call, we won't get in trouble. But if something does happen, we'll still have the cell phone with us."

"1:15?" Colin asked.

"I'm pretty sure I had the vision at 1:38," I said. "I think that's what time it was on my alarm clock."

Colin rubbed his hands together. "This is going to be awesome! We're going to save someone tonight. I almost feel like I need a costume or something." He looked around the room. "Do you have a cape I could borrow?"

Lisa and I didn't share in Colin's enthusiasm. "C'mon, guys," he said. "This is going to work. I know it. Plus, this is shaping up to be the most exciting birthday party ever."

"Thanks," I said. "Just wait till you see the goodie-bags. I have some fortune cookies that tell you when you're going to die."

Lisa shivered. "That would be creepy."

"Yeah," I said. "Tell me about it."

After dinner, my parents made us watch a movie about a kid who never grew up, a Peter-Pan-type story, only without the green unitard and pixie dust. I'm sure I would have hated it if I had paid any attention. But my mind was on Mr. Utlet. What if he was *already* dying? What if he had mixed up his medications and it was already too late for me to help him? No... something told me the incident we'd be trying to stop would be sudden. No one screams like that unless there's some major trauma.

"What did you think?" my mom asked.

The movie was over, and I hadn't even noticed. I snapped back to reality, watching the credits roll across the screen. "It was great, Mom. Thanks." I stood and moved to the base of the stairs. "It must have been hard to find a movie that Colin hasn't seen."

Colin winced. "Yeah, I actually hadn't seen that one. It was really... er... good?"

"Did you guys see the symbolism in the story?" my dad asked. "How the boy's teacher died, and he coped and became stronger because of it?"

So that's why he had insisted we watch this film. I should have expected it: who but my dad would turn movie night into an opportunity to talk about Mrs. Farnsworthy's death? His bringing it up again only made me feel worse, though. And since my dad made his living reading people, he didn't miss my reaction.

"Son, there's nothing wrong with having confusing feelings about death. If you'd like to talk to me about this— about anything at all—I'm here for you." He placed his hand in my mom's and added, "We're both here for you."

"I know, Dad. Thanks."

"I think we're just tired, Mr. Curse," Lisa said, standing up suddenly. "It's been a really long day."

Colin did the worst fake stretch I'd ever seen and added, "Yeah, I'm beat."

"Where did you kids want to sleep?"

"Outside," I said, sounding a bit too eager.

My mom winced. She wasn't a fan of anything outdoors—especially sleeping in it. "Really? I didn't think you liked the outdoors."

"What? I love it," I said.

"Yeah, right!" Becky said from over my shoulder. "You practically cried when we went camping last summer. You hate sleeping outdoors."

"Actually I just hate sleeping outdoors with *you*," I said. She was right, though. I took after my mom in that regard. Becky put her hand on her hip and cocked an eyebrow. I sneered back. "It's tough to enjoy the great outdoors when you have a giant ball of hair blocking your view of the stars."

"Argh!" She marched forward, kicked me in the shins, and then stomped up the stairs to her room. I hopped back to the couch and rubbed where my sister had kicked me. *Brat.*

"I told you not to tease her about her hair, Dean," Mom scolded.

"She gave you fair warning, champ," my dad added, patting me on the shoulder. "Okay, kids, Dean knows where the sleeping bags are. If you need anything, just holler."

"Thanks, Dad," I groaned.

"Come on, Dean," Colin said once my parents had left the room. "No one's going to believe that you killed a couple of muggers if your little sister can knock you off your feet."

"She's stronger than she looks," I grumbled.

Lisa shook her head. "You really shouldn't tease her about her hair. It's clearly a sore spot."

Colin laughed. "So you'd hit a guy if he made fun of your hair?"

She took a step toward Colin. "Are you saying there's something funny about my hair?"

Colin swallowed and shuffled back a step.

"Good. But if you had something nasty to say about my hair, I wouldn't kick you in the shins."

"I didn't think so."

"I'd hit you somewhere else. And I'd use my knee."

We finished setting up outside by eleven, and the light in my parent's bedroom window turned off by midnight.

"Okay," Lisa said. "Let's go."

"Just like that?" I said. "We just walk across the street and start peeping through the windows?"

"You have a better plan?"

"Um... no, I just wanted to make sure we were on the same page."

"C'mon, guys," Colin said, already halfway across the lawn. "Let's go save this old geezer."

CHAPTER 15

We crept across the street and into Mr. Utlet's backyard. Colin was a bit more excited than I would have liked. He kept pouncing behind trees and rolling across the grass. But once we made it to the house, he calmed down a bit. We crouched behind a shrub at the back of Mr. Utlet's house and peered through the partially drawn curtains hanging over a large picture window.

"I can't see anything," Colin said. "Do you guys see anything?"

"We need a better view," I said.

Lisa gestured toward the backdoor at the other corner of the house. "Colin, go look in those windows over there, and Dean, you go around the front. If you see anything suspicious, come back here."

"Who died and made you boss?" Colin grumbled.

Lisa gave him a stern look and he stalked off, sliding his back along the stucco wall. I gulped back a feeling of dread that had taken post in my throat, and moved toward the front of the house. The moon wasn't full, but it still cast a bluish light that seemed too bright for what we were doing. Even plastering myself against the house, I felt exposed. There just weren't enough shadows. I kept imagining one of the neighbors—blue-haired Mrs. Barton, perhaps—poking her head out a bedroom window and catching us peeping into old man Utlet's windows. They'd call the cops for sure, and what would we say? *"Oh, we were just looking in to see if he was still alive."* Yeah, they wouldn't have a problem with that explanation.

I peered around the corner and thought I heard a muffled grumble. I braved another step, then another, following the noise. While I was kneeling on a bed of perennials at the other end of the house, I noticed that a small window just above my head was open a crack and the grumbling was coming from inside. Only it didn't sound like grumbling anymore—it sounded as if someone were choking or struggling for breath.

No longer worried if anyone could see me, I jumped up and pressed my face to the glass. The blinds were only half drawn, and the moonlight cast a soft glow over Mr. Utlet's body. He was lying flat on his bed, wearing the same clothes we'd seen him in earlier; a brown book lay open on his chest. The noise coming from him was ungodly. I opened my mouth to shout for Colin to call an ambulance, sure Mr. Utlet was suffering from some kind of seizure, until he turned to his side and smacked his lips.

Snoring? He's snoring?

I stared down at the old man, disturbed and relieved in the same instant. On the one hand, the fact that he was obviously alive relieved me, but on the other hand, the fact that any human being could sound as if they had swallowed a chainsaw and still be considered okay was something I had trouble wrapping my head around. I probably would have stood there for the rest of the night if Lisa hadn't come out of nowhere and tackled me into the bushes.

"Shhhh!" Lisa pressed a finger to her lips. Her eyes were the size of grenades, and she looked on the verge of panic. I opened my mouth to speak, but she shook her head quickly and pointed over my shoulder.

I turned and stared back across the manicured lawn. It was as empty as it had been when we arrived. I didn't see anything particularly strange... But then a movement at the edge of the lawn caught my eye. Two men clad in dark clothing rounded the corner of the house and moved toward the front porch. My heart jumped into my throat while my mind struggled to make sense of what was happening.

A robbery?

I risked a glance at my watch. 12:46. We still had almost an hour before... well, before whatever was going to happen would happen. *They'll try the door, it'll be locked, and they'll move on.* At least I hoped they would.

The leaves to my right rustled, and Lisa tightened her grip on my arm. A third man stepped out from the bushes only a couple feet away. He was about thirty, or maybe late twenties, and had a shaved head and a mean scowl. He was close enough that I could see the tattoo on his forearm: an eagle landing on a sword. All he had to do was look to his right and he'd spot us, but his eyes stayed glued to the house. He strode across the lawn as though he had all the right in the world to be there, unconcerned that he was in plain sight of anyone who happened to be watching from surrounding homes, and reached for the door at the top of the porch. I held my breath as he turned the knob and pushed the door.

Locked, thank God.

He gestured to the other two men, signaling them to go around opposite ends of the house. One man moved toward us in a half crouch, shifting back and forth like some caveman cat burglar. His head was the shape of a partially deflated football, and his skin was pasty white. When he got to Mr. Utlet's bedroom window, he paused and poked his head above the sill. It was then that I realized the yard had become silent. No noises at all. Mr. Utlet had stopped snoring.

The man hovered on the stoop for a moment, taking stock of the homes across the street, seemingly searching for any sign that he'd been spotted, before making his way around the corner and down the side of the house. When he got halfway down, he stopped next to another window, peered inside, and then shoved something under the pane. The wood groaned and a second later the window was open and the man had hoisted himself inside. I turned back to the front of the house. The man with the tattoo was kneeling before the door and using something that looked like a very narrow screwdriver to mess with the lock.

So this was how it was going to go down: a bunch of burglars would rob an old man, kill him, and for what? Some old war medals? A giant coffee tin filled with pennies?

But we still had time. We could stop it.

"Call 911," I whispered over my shoulder. Lisa didn't budge.

I turned. Lisa was eyeing the man on the porch as though her gaze could turn him to dust. "Hey," I nudged her with my elbow, "call the police."

"Don't you have the phone?" she whispered.

"No," I whispered. "Where's Colin?"

I heard a creak and glanced back at the porch just in time to see the man disappear through the front door.

"Where's Colin?" I repeated, more desperately this time.

Lisa turned to the house, then back to me. "I don't know. He was at the back. We saw those... those goons creeping across the lawn." She looked down the side of the house. "The backdoor wasn't locked, and Colin opened it to see if he could hear anything." She jumped to her feet. "Oh, no. He must be inside. I'll bet you anything he's inside."

I grabbed her before she could run to the house. "Go back to my place and call 911." She hesitated and opened her mouth to argue, but I cut her off. "I'll help Colin, but I can't do it alone. And you're the fastest." If there was ever something we needed in a hurry, Lisa was the one to get it. There was a section on her bedroom wall covered in so many track and field ribbons you'd think someone had splashed a can of blue paint on the wall.

"Be careful," she whispered and then sprinted off toward my house.

I clenched my fists at my side and tried to get my breathing under control. I couldn't help the first two people I had seen in my visions. And I wasn't able to help Mrs. Farnsworthy. But Mr. Utlet... I was going to help him. He wasn't going to die. I checked my watch. 1:03. I had time. He wasn't going to die.

I crouched low and made my way toward the door. That's when I heard the first gunshot. The second shot rang out when I opened the door.

CHAPTER 16

I burst through the door and rushed down an empty hallway. I heard scuffles from a room just up ahead and then a crash. I rounded the corner and rushed into the living room, not entirely sure what I was going to find, but afraid it would be Mr. Utlet bleeding to death.

My mouth dropped when I finally saw what was going on. Mr. Utlet wasn't shot. Instead, he stood over two of the men, one of whom was lying prone beneath chunks of porcelain and an overturned end table. The other, the man with the football-shaped head, was shuffling away from the old man, trying to prop himself against the wall. A bullet-sized hole in his right pant leg oozed blood.

"You! What are you doing here?" Mr. Utlet barked at me.

"I... we... " I blinked, trying to make sense of the scene before me. "You did this?"

"They started it," Mr. Utlet said, defending himself. He waved an object that took me a moment to identify as a gun. "This isn't my gun." He kicked the unconscious man at his feet. "This numbskull brought it. Bet you're regretting that, aren't ya, genius?" He looked back at me. "That doesn't explain what you're doing here."

"We were... um... trying to help you."

"We? We who?"

"Colin and L—"

"Put the gun down, old man."

The voice came from my right, and without thinking, I jumped to my left and ducked behind a ratty old armchair. The man with the tattoo gripped Colin by the shoulder and pressed a knife against his neck. He sneered at me and then turned back to Mr. Utlet.

"Put it down!" he said again.

"I don't think so." Mr. Utlet straightened his arms, pointed the gun at the burglar's head, and narrowed his eyes.

The tattooed man flexed his arm around Colin's neck and shifted the hand that held the blade. Colin whimpered as a single bead of red trickled down his throat.

"Drop the gun, old man. Or I'll shove the blade straight through this little brat's neck."

Mr. Utlet's mouth twitched, and the muscles in his jaw clenched. I was sure he was about to take a shot, but at the last second he dropped the gun to the floor and gave it a little kick so it slid under his couch. "Let the kid go."

The burglar moved the knife away from Colin's neck but kept a grip on his shoulder. He turned to the man propped up against the wall. "Darren, you okay?"

"He shot me in the leg," the man moaned. "I can't walk."

"Do it anyway," tattoo man ordered. "What about Jim?" He nodded at the man lying still on the floor.

"The old man bashed him over the head and took his gun."

The man with the tattoo shoved Colin, sending him sprawling to the floor, and then moved toward his fallen comrade and nudged him with his foot. "Jim! Jim, get up." Tattoo man's buddy didn't even move a finger.

Colin scrambled across the hardwood floor and took a post next to me behind the arm-chair. He kept one hand pressed to his neck.

"Get out of my house," Mr. Utlet warned.

"Tell us where you keep your money, and we'll gladly leave."

"What money?"

"Don't play games, old man. We've been doing this long enough to know that all you old suckers keep wads of cash in your house."

Mr. Utlet's eyes became slits. "Get out of my house."

"Or what?" Tattoo man flicked the knife in front of his face. "I have the—"

Mr. Utlet moved like a jackrabbit. One second he was standing two or three yards from the burglar, and the next, his fist was connecting with the other man's jaw. His punch only managed to knock the man back a step, but the knife clattered to the floor. Tattoo man growled and swung back at Mr. Utlet. I blinked, and the next thing I knew, the two of them were on the ground rolling on top of each other, fists connecting so fast the room filled with sounds like a gorilla beating its chest. Somehow the tattooed man managed to stand up and kick Mr. Utlet while he was down. Mr. Utlet groaned, then lashed out with his foot and connected with the inside of the robber's knee with a resounding *crack*. The man howled and staggered back, knocking into a floor lamp. Colin and I shielded our eyes as it smashed to the floor. Opaque shards of glass scattered around the room. Mr. Utlet was on his feet again. He slammed his fist into the man's ribs, and as the burglar staggered back, Mr. Utlet tackled him.

"Get the gun!" the tattooed man yelled.

The guy with the hole in his leg pulled himself to his feet and hobbled toward the couch. I could hear sirens in the distance. Help was on its way, but it wasn't coming fast enough.

I glanced at the ratty old armchair we were hiding behind, then at the man with the bloody leg, then back at the chair. "Push," I said to Colin. Together, we pushed the armchair with our shoulders and launched it toward the man like some upholstered battering ram. His eyes widened, and he tried to move, but his injured leg didn't allow it. We struck him fullon and knocked him back. He staggered, arms circling the air like blades on a broken windmill, until finally he crashed through the large picture window and thudded to the ground below.

We risked a peek over the ledge. His eyes were closed, and he was wrapped in Mr. Utlet's paisley curtains like an Egyptian mummy that had insisted on being wrapped in trendy bandages.

"Move!" Mr. Utlet yelled from behind us. He had the tattooed man's arm twisted in an unnatural position, and he was running him toward the window.

Colin and I dove to the side just as Mr. Utlet tossed the burglar through. His feet clipped the ledge and he landed with a crunch atop his friend. Police cars and emergency vehicles careened to our block and drove over the sidewalk right onto Mr. Utlet's lawn, headlights suddenly brightening the living room.

Mr. Utlet limped to the couch, shoved it aside, and plucked up the revolver. He looked at us and a fleck of amusement played across his face. "I haven't had that much fun since Beirut." He nodded toward our armchair battering ram. "Quick thinking, boys. Nicely done."

He took a couple steps forward. I thought he was going to shake our hands or maybe pat us on the back. I didn't find out because as soon as he stepped in front of the window and into the white beams of the police car headlights, we heard, "Freeze! Drop the gun!"

That's when all the color from the room bled away. Just like before, everything grayed and that feeling of undeniable dread engulfed me.

Mr. Utlet smiled. "They think I'm the bad guy." He turned to the window and raised his empty hand to his forehead, shielding his eyes from the lights. "Now see here!" he yelled. "These boys and I... " He gestured toward us and then froze.

In the seconds before it happened, I saw what the officers were seeing from their positions behind the cruisers. I felt like I should run to Mr. Utlet and throw my hands out like a human shield to protect him. Instead, I didn't move a muscle, frozen by fear and uncertainty, and watched my worst nightmare come true.

Since his free hand was shielding his eyes from the headlights, the hand he used to make his gesture was the one holding the gun. To the police, it looked as though he were taking aim at a couple of unfortunate kids. What happened next sounded as if someone had set a row of fire-crackers aflame. Mr. Utlet jerked and twitched in time to the bursts of noise. Then he dropped to the floor, and a shallow gray pool formed under his bullet-riddled body. As color filled the world again, the pool turned blood red.

I took in a raspy breath as I looked down at my wristwatch.

"One thirty-eight," I choked. "It's 1:38."

CHAPTER 17

I didn't leave my house for days. Lisa and Colin called from time to time, but I couldn't bring myself to talk to them. I'd known *exactly* what time Mr. Utlet would die, right to the minute. All I had to do was stop it. I should've called the police a few minutes earlier, or made a ruckus on the front lawn to scare those men away, or at least made them think that Mr. Utlet wouldn't be an easy target. I went over and over all the ways the night could have played out differently. Each new possibility depressed me more than the last.

My dad used his connections in the psychology community to pull some strings with the school board. Lisa, Colin, and I were excused from our final exams and given a pass into grade ten—not that I really cared. But we also had to attend group and one-on-one counseling. I'd already missed two sessions of both, but my parents were forcing me to go to the next group session.

According to Dad, Lisa and Colin hadn't missed a session and seemed to be doing well. Apparently, quite a few kids were having a tough time with the accident at school and were in counseling as well. Eric Feldman was among them. I was pretty sure Eric just wanted to be excused from his exams. Not that I could blame him, I guess. If I hadn't been so devastated by what had happened to Mr. Utlet and Mrs. Farnsworthy, I'd have been overjoyed.

The only good thing to happen over those few days was what *didn't* happen: no more visions. No more screaming faces, no more shrieks of terror. Whatever nightmare I had been plunged into seemed to have ended. For now.

I was brooding in bed, wondering if the past few days had been some test that I had failed, when there was a knock at my bedroom door.

"Honey?" my mom called. "Colin and Lisa are with me. Can they come in?"

I closed my eyes. Inhaled. Exhaled. I had avoided my friends long enough. Sooner or later, I knew they'd come find me. I cleared my throat, pushed myself out of bed, and opened the door.

"Hey, guys." They were both dressed in nice clothing as if they were on their way to church. Colin was wearing a button-up shirt, which made him look ten times dressier than I'd ever seen him, and Lisa had on a dark knee-length dress. A newspaper was tucked under her arm.

"How're you doing, man?" Colin asked.

"Better," I lied.

"You don't look better," Colin said. He swept past me into the room, followed by Lisa, who shut the door behind her. "There was nothing we could've done." He poked at some of the stuff on my desk.

"Whatever."

"We did everything we could," Lisa said.

I reddened. *Had they planned the speech before getting here?* "What do you mean we did everything we could? We killed him. *I* killed him."

Lisa scrunched up her face. "Don't be stupid."

"If he hadn't pointed that gun at us, he wouldn't have been shot."

"Not by the cops, maybe," Colin said, "but probably by the robbers."

"No! That's just it, Colin. He'd already beaten two of the robbers. He had the gun. He only put it down because the third guy had a knife on you."

Lisa and Colin looked at each other with raised brows.

"It's because we were there that he died."

"I don't believe that," Lisa said flatly. "No. It's not possible."

"I'm the common denominator, guys. I'm the reason for all these deaths."

"Oh yeah?" Colin asked. "And how exactly are you responsible for Mrs. Farnsworthy's death?"

"She wasn't standing behind her desk, right?" I widened my eyes at Lisa, waiting for a response.

She put her fists on her hips and leaned forward. "Yeah, so?"

"If she'd been standing behind her desk, she probably wouldn't have been killed. And the reason she wasn't standing behind her desk was because *I* said there was a rat hiding under her desk."

"Oh God, Dean!" Lisa took a step back and looked up at the ceiling. "People believed you for about five minutes. After that, no one believed that stupid rat story. No one. Not the other students and certainly not Mrs. Farnsworthy."

I waved my hand dismissively. "This curse doesn't make me see death so I can stop it. It makes me bring death. I attract it. I'm a... I'm a *harbinger of death*. Come near me and you're marked." Colin shuffled back a step as I pointed a warning finger at him. "That's right. Stay away. I'm like one of those guys who walks through the forest spray painting big red Xs on all the trees that are going to be chopped down." When I finished, I was breathing so heavily you'd have thought I'd just run a marathon.

After a lengthy pause, Lisa said, "Wow."

"What?"

"Nothing. I didn't realize that the world revolved around you. That's all. Impressive." She turned to Colin. "Don't you think that's impressive?" She didn't wait for his reply before turning back to me and adding, "*Harbinger*, eh? Yeah, that has a pretty good ring to it."

"Shuddup," I muttered.

"Oh, get over yourself, Dean. You're no more the harbinger of death than Colin is the harbinger of intelligence."

"Hey!" Colin said. "I'm right here, you know? I can hear you."

Lisa grabbed my hand with both of hers. "You're not doing this, Dean. It's not you. Something is happening *to you*, not *by you*." She kept my hand in hers for a few moments before releasing it and adding, "Now get dressed. We have a funeral to attend."

I swallowed hard and asked, though I really didn't want to know, "Whose funeral?"

"Mr. Vidmar's dead," Lisa said softly. "He died the same day we stopped in to see him."

I lowered myself to the edge of my bed and dropped my head in my hands.

Lisa rolled her eyes. "That doesn't mean it's your fault!" she continued. "But this is important. We need to go to the funeral."

"Show him the article," Colin prodded.

I glanced up. "What article?"

"It's his obituary." Lisa opened the paper and smoothed it out beside me. She tapped the center of the page. "Here. Look who it says he's survived by."

The obituary was barely a paragraph long, and Mr. Vidmar's brother's name jumped out at me. "Dmitri." The name gave me a chill as it rolled off my tongue.

"Dmitri," Colin echoed. "That's who Mr. Vidmar said we needed to talk to, remember?"

"You didn't get any answers from Mr. Vidmar," Lisa said. "But it sounds like his brother knows something."

I sat motionless for a moment. Part embarrassed, part terrified, part relieved. "I'm sorry about my little freak-out there."

"Hey," Colin said, "don't worry about it." He walked over and put his arm around my shoulders and led me to my closet. "But you might actually want to keep that nickname. The Harbinger sounds freaking awesome!"

I smiled, and I didn't have to force myself to either. It was good to have my friends nearby, and it was good to know they didn't think I was a walking death trap. "I'm actually not having the visions anymore."

Colin and Lisa looked at each other and then back at me.

"You're not having the visions *right now*," Lisa corrected. "That doesn't mean they won't come back."

I sighed. I had avoided considering that possibility, but I knew she was right. If these visions came back, it would be nice to know if there was a way to stop them. Or maybe understand what I'd done to deserve them. Something, anything. If it was a curse, perhaps there was a way to get rid of it.

"Okay," I said. "Help me find some clothes."

To my surprise, my dad thought that going to the funeral was a brilliant idea and immediately agreed to drive us. "First step to recovery is acceptance," he said. Acceptance was the last thought on my mind. Answers, that's what I wanted. That was the only thing that would help. According to the obituary, the service was supposed to start at two. We told my dad we wanted to go a bit early so we could express our condolences before everyone else got there, so we arrived at the church just after one.

My dad offered to come in and sit with us, but given our true purpose, I thought that wouldn't be the best idea. He told us to call him when we were ready to be picked up.

The church looked as though someone had thrown a cross on a newly condemned building and decided to call it a place of worship. There was a sign outside, but either the letters had been written upside down or the writing wasn't in English. We walked up the narrow path and ducked through the doorway. A dozen or so pews lined either side of the chapel. Up front, a piano stood on one side of an elevated stage. On the other side, there was a human-sized box. Except for the man sitting in the front pew, staring at the casket, we were all alone.

I took a deep breath, prepared myself for the worst, and stepped into the aisle.

CHAPTER 18

Inside the chapel, the man turned in his seat and glanced questioningly down the aisle at us. He had close-cropped hair, the same color as Mr. Vidmar's, and wore a white button-up shirt with a narrow black tie and a black leather jacket.

Colin nudged me forward. "Say something."

We shuffled nervously to the front of the church.

I cleared my throat. "Dmitri Vidmar?"

Dark crescents marred the skin under his eyes and two days of stubble accented his pale skin. He stood as we neared, his eyes narrowing in scrutiny. "I wondered if you'd come," he said. "You're that kid who saved my brother."

Saved his brother? My eyes flashed to the coffin at the front of the room. *Obviously not.* "I'm Dean, sir, Dean Curse. These are my friends, Lisa and Colin."

Dmitri gestured to the pew behind him. "Have a seat."

"We're really sorry about your brother," Lisa said as she slid into the pew. "He seemed like a nice man."

"Thank you." His gaze never left my face. "The nurses at the hospital told me you three visited him on the day he died."

I nodded.

"I was out of the country." He hung his head. "I was trying to get here before... I didn't want him to be alone when he died."

A brief silence passed. "He mentioned you," Colin said finally.

Dmitri looked up and smiled. "Did he?"

"Yes, sir," I said.

"I wish I had been there." His gaze lingered on the coffin before turning back to me. "What did he say?"

"Sir." My palms were wet and I wiped them off on my pants. "He said I should ask you to tell me about Preepyad."

Dmitri blinked. "What?"

I glanced at Colin and Lisa, who both nodded in encouragement. "Pree-pi-yad," I repeated slowly, trying to pronounce each syllable the way Mr. Vidmar had. "He said to ask you about it."

"Why the heck would he say that?" his voice took on an angry edge and he shook his head. "Nothing good can come from talking about that. No. My brother's dead, I won't have the memory of him tarnished with that story or his association with those people."

I cleared my throat. "Sir, when I helped your brother in the alley... um... he... well... he said—"

"I'm sure I can guess what my brother said to you," Dmitri interrupted.

"You can?"

He nodded. "And I'm sorry. He wasn't well."

"He wasn't?" Colin prodded.

Dmitri shifted in his seat and rubbed his palms on his jeans. "Listen, my brother was a good man. I'm grateful that you came to his aid. After everything my brother's been through, all the time he spent with psychiatrists, all the injuries, all the suicide—" He caught himself mid-sentence and flushed, seemingly embarrassed that he'd let his words get away from himself.

"Sir," I said, "what is it you think your brother said to me?"

"No doubt he told you that you were going to die."

I gasped, and Dmitri looked confused. "Isn't that what he said? He says it to a lot of people."

"N... no, sir. He only said 'glimpse.'"

"Glimpse?"

"That's right."

Dmitri looked thoughtfully at the ceiling for a moment. "Are you sure that's what he said?"

"Completely sure, sir. Do you know what that means?"

Lisa and Colin leaned in.

"No," Dmitri answered.

"*No?*" Colin rocked back in the pew.

"Colin, be quiet," Lisa hushed.

"No, I won't be quiet. We need some answers." Colin turned back to Dmitri. "Sir, I'm sorry about your loss, but something's happening to my friend here, and we're pretty sure your brother cursed him in some way."

"Cursed him?" Dmitri stood up and straightened his jacket. "Did you just say that my brother *cursed* your friend? Are you suggesting he was some kind of witch?"

"N... no, sir," Lisa said. "Dean's just been having some difficulties lately, and they seem to have started after your brother's attack."

Dmitri regarded us for a few moments as if trying to work out if we were being serious or not. "What kind of problems?"

"He's seeing things," Colin answered.

He shook his head. "Don't tell me you three are part of that stupid cult too."

"Cult?" Lisa stiffened. "What cult? We're not part of any cult."

"Cult, society, organization, whatever you want to call it. I shouldn't be surprised that they would stoop to recruiting kids." He turned to me and spoke through clenched teeth. "Let me guess. You have visions of people who have twenty-four hours to live, right?"

I gulped and managed a quick nod.

Dmitri's face reddened. "You think this is some kind of joke?" he exploded. "Those Patronus psychos ruined my brother's life! They're the reason he's dead. I couldn't protect my brother from them when he was alive, but I am going to make sure he's safe from them now." He gestured furiously toward the door. "Get out. Now!"

Dmitri's expression flicked between rage and grief, and I was pretty sure with one more word from any of us he'd have a meltdown. I nodded, grabbed Lisa and Colin by the arms, and pulled them out of the pew and down the aisle. "We didn't mean any disrespect," I said. "I'm sorry."

"Out!"

We rushed out of the church and didn't stop running until we were around the corner.

"What a psycho!" Colin said once we were a safe distance.

"His brother just died," Lisa said. "Give the guy a break."

"A break?" Colin straightened up. "You're nuts. He looked like he wanted us in caskets." He unknotted his tie and threw it on the ground. "What a waste of time. We didn't learn anything, and now an angry Russian probably wants us dead."

"What do you mean we didn't learn anything?" Lisa

shook her head. "Weren't you listening to him?" Lisa didn't give him a chance to respond before continuing. "First"—she lifted a finger—"we know that there's something called a Patronus Cult or Society or something like that. Second, Mr. Vidmar was locked up for some kind of mental illness, which I remember reading in his hospital records." She paused and looked off to the right as if considering something, and then turned back to Colin and added, "And third, it sounds like Mr. Vidmar was seeing the same things as Dean. I think that's pretty important stuff."

"Why?" Colin demanded to know.

"Because, Colin, if you're right and this is a curse, maybe someone gave it to Mr. Vidmar, and maybe the visions were the cause of his illness."

"We learned something else too," I added reluctantly. I didn't really share Lisa's excitement about our visit with Dmitri, and some of what we had learned was downright frightening. "I think Mr. Vidmar tried to commit suicide. You two heard him in there, didn't you?" I wondered how many more screaming twisting faces I'd have to see before I went nuts too.

They nodded.

"He's not you, Dean. That won't happen to you." Lisa placed her hand on my arm. "And at least now we have a place to start. Don't you think so?"

"I'll tell you what we need to do," Colin said a little too enthusiastically. "We need to get rid of that curse and we need to do it quick."

"Yeah," Lisa sneered. "And how do you propose we do that?"

"Easy." Colin turned to me. "Mr. Vidmar said he gave you the curse, right? So maybe that's all you need to do. Just go find someone and give it to them. Just think it in your head, 'I give you this curse,' and that's it!"

"That's the stupidest thing I've ever heard," Lisa said.

Colin ignored her and added, "You said the guy whispered, 'Glimpse,' right?" He didn't wait for me to respond. "So you should do that too."

"And what if it's like a cold, Colin?" Lisa said with a huff.

"What do you mean?"

"I can give you my cold by sneezing on you but I don't lose mine."

Colin chewed his lip for a moment, and then shook his head. "That's not how curses work."

"We don't know for sure that it's a curse—it might be something else entirely."

While Colin and Lisa continued arguing, the horror of my situation set in. Like Mr. Vidmar, I'd slowly go crazy. I'd probably spend my life locked away in some padded room. And when I did get out, I'd be so nuts I might just try to kill myself too. My stomach flipped, and cold beads of sweat formed on my forehead.

I shoved past Colin and Lisa to the edge of the sidewalk and vomited in a bed of daisies.

CHAPTER 19

Lisa offered me a Kleenex from her pocket and placed a gentle hand on my shoulder while Colin laced his fingers behind his head and paced along a section of the sidewalk. "Pull it together, Dean," he said. "We can do this. In fact, we can do this right now." He gestured down the street as I wiped my mouth. "There's a group of people over there. Go grab one of them, concentrate on giving up the curse, and say, 'Glimpse.'"

"You really think it's going to be that easy?"

He shrugged. "Isn't it worth a try?"

"And how exactly is he going to know that it worked?" Lisa asked.

"I guess he won't have any more *visions* now, will he?"

"Great idea, Colin. You really thought that one through, didn't you? And let's say your little plan works. What then? Is it even *fair* to pass something like this to someone else?"

"It's not like he had a choice in the matter. Why should he care if someone else does?"

"Stop it, guys," I said. "Lisa, do you have another idea?" Part of me wanted to take Colin's suggestion and run with it, but another part of me agreed that it wasn't fair. If a drug dealer had walked by at that very moment, or some other criminal-type, I'd probably have tried. But if Lisa was right, if it could be like a cold or virus or something, then maybe I'd just be giving more people the same problem as me. That wouldn't help anyone.

"Yeah, as a matter of fact, I do." She turned, shielded her eyes with the butt of her hand, and looked down the street. "We're not far from the library. I think we should go there."

"Why?" Colin said. "We're out of school. We passed, remember?"

Lisa sighed and rolled her eyes. "So we can figure this out. There's bound to be something in the library about that secret society. The library computers have different databases. You can search stuff on their computers that you can't get without a subscription."

"You're right," I said. "I remember my dad talking about that once. That's where we should start. We find out how to get rid of this curse." Lisa looked at me nervously, and I added, "Preferably without passing it on to someone else. Otherwise... " I started, reaching out for Colin.

He realized what I was doing and screamed, "Don't

touch me!" He staggered back, eyes wide, and dove into the bushes. Lisa and I laughed when we realized he very nearly landed in my vomit.

After three hours in the library we weren't any closer to understanding the mysterious Patronus Society. Except that the word Patronus wasn't Russian—it was Latin. It meant protection. The Protection Society. Colin thought "society" didn't sound dangerous enough and wanted us to refer to it as a cult. "It has a better ring to it," he said. "Plus, it's what Dmitri called it." It really didn't matter. Society, cult... both terms produced the same number of results. Zero. We used the computers, searched the databases, and even had the librarian help us search the archives for any mention of the society in newspapers or journal articles. Each time, our searches returned blank. We even tried to search for Preepyad— Google corrected our spelling to Pripyat—but we only learned that it was the name of some teeny-tiny town in Russia. No mention of any society or cult. If the Patronus Society existed, they'd done a wonderful job of keeping it secret.

"It doesn't make sense," Lisa said. "If Dmitri knew about them, then others should too. There should be a record of it."

"Unless it doesn't exist," I said.

Colin and Lisa looked confused.

"If the society did exist, we'd have found something, at least some obscure reference to indicate it was real. Let's face it... maybe Mr. Vidmar was nuts."

Lisa shook her head. "He wasn't crazy, Dean." She glanced at Colin and then back to me. "You had visions of people, people who died exactly twenty-four hours later. Your visions came true. There's nothing crazy about that. It's miraculous. Not crazy."

"I agree," Colin said. "We're just missing something."

"Shush!" A young woman wearing a dark skirt and button-up sweater was suddenly towering above us. The gold lettering on her name badge identified her as a librarian, and the tiny cart of books at her side confirmed it. She didn't look like any librarian I'd ever seen. With her high ponytail and perfect row of white teeth, she looked like she could've been a cheerleader—well, an angry cheerleader who hated noise. She leaned over our table. "If you're going to have your little fantasy club meetings in the library, you're going to have to keep your voices down. Understand?"

"Fantasy club?" Lisa looked offended. "This isn't a fantasy club."

The librarian waved her hand dismissively. "Well,

whatever you're doing, keep your voices down. The rest of the library doesn't need to hear about your visions of dead people or secret societies."

Lisa huffed, then glanced at her watch. "We were just leaving anyway."

We stood, and something to the right caught my eye. A sudden movement. I turned just as a sleeve of dark leather disappeared behind one of the shelves. I caught a glimpse of a figure—he seemed familiar, but I couldn't figure out why. I was about to go investigate when Lisa tugged my arm. "C'mon. Let's go."

I felt completely defeated while we waited outside the library. We had come looking for answers, and it seemed the only thing I had was even more questions. Nothing made sense.

I called my dad, and he showed up about ten minutes later.

"How'd it go?" he asked as we piled into the car.

I shrugged. "Fine."

"How was Mr. Vidmar's brother doing?"

I couldn't think of anything good that would come from telling my dad about Dmitri freaking out, so I lied. "As well as could be expected."

"His brother thanked us for coming," Lisa added.

"Oh, good," my dad said. "I'm sure it meant a lot to him." He looked in the rearview mirror. "What were you guys doing in the library?"

"We were looking for information on the Protection Society," Colin said.

My dad's eyebrows rose. "The what?"

It was a good thing Colin wasn't sitting beside me or I'd have punched him. "It's nothing," I said. "It's just some make-believe secret society that Mr. Vidmar thought he was a part of. We wanted to see if it might have been true."

Dad nodded. "I understand exactly," he said. "You shared a very traumatic experience with that man. It's perfectly natural that you'd like to know more about him." He raised his brows. "Did you find anything?"

"Nope," Lisa said. "Not a thing."

"I'm not surprised," my dad said.

"Why? Because he was crazy?" My voice had a sharp edge, and I sounded a lot angrier than I had intended. My face flushed.

"Um, no," my father said. "I'm not surprised because that library doesn't have very many books on cultural anthropology or religious studies."

"On what?" Colin asked.

"Cultural anthropology or religious studies," he repeated. "There's an entire section dedicated to those fields at the university library." He glanced at me. "Making sense of things at a time like this is important,

Dean. I'm pleased you're searching for answers. But if you want to learn about secret societies, if you think that will help you cope, then you should try the university library."

My eyes widened. "Could you take us?"

"I'm working tomorrow," he said. "You kids could come along if you want."

"Yeah, that would be great." I turned and looked in the back seat. Lisa was smiling and nodding. Only Colin looked confused.

He cocked his head and looked past me, toward my dad. "You have class during the summer?"

"Classes run all year long," he said. "Sometimes it's people trying to finish their degree faster. Sometimes students who failed a course try to do it again during the summer so they don't delay their degree."

"That's just wrong," Colin said.

Lisa smiled sweetly. "Don't worry, Colin. I'm sure you'll learn all about summer school before you graduate high school."

While Lisa and Colin bickered, I tried to look on the bright side. We still had a chance to find out what was happening to me. I just hoped that whatever I learned at the university library tomorrow would help, not condemn me for life.

CHAPTER 20

The public library was big—several times larger than the high school library—but as we stepped into the university library, our jaws dropped. Row upon row of shelved books stretched out farther than I could see. To the right was a staircase that led up to another *two* floors of books.

"Are you kids going to be all right?" my dad asked. When we didn't answer, he gestured to a large doughnut-shaped desk in the middle of the room. A young man with a serious expression and brown plastic-rimmed glasses pointed students in various directions as if he were directing traffic at some busy intersection. "If you have questions, go ask the librarian. He should be able to point you in the right direction, and he'll be happy to help you."

I looked over at the man again just as he smashed a rubber stamp against a hardcover. He didn't look too happy to me.

My dad checked his watch. "It's 10:45. I have a quick meeting with the dean, and then I'll be in my office grading papers until you guys are ready to go. Okay?"

Still coming to terms with the size of the library, I only managed to nod in reply.

"Good luck." He turned and headed back out the doors.

"This is huge," Colin gasped. "Really, really, really huge."

"Oh, c'mon, you guys," Lisa said. She grabbed our wrists and dragged us to the growing line at the librarian's desk.

The line moved quickly, and before we knew it, we were standing beneath the stern glare of the librarian. His head was the shape of an egg. His glasses were thick, and they magnified his eyes to at least three times their regular size so they looked like bloodshot pancakes.

I heard Colin gasp at my right. "He looks like an alien," he muttered to himself.

"I'm not an alien," the man growled.

Colin yelped and took a quick step behind my shoulder.

"We're looking for information on secret societies," Lisa said, obviously trying to ignore Colin. "Particularly the Patronus Society. Though it may be called the Patronus Cult."

The librarian kept his gaze on Colin for a couple of extra seconds before turning to his computer. "Hmm."

He scratched his chin and tapped the keys on the computer. Then he tapped the keys again, and then again, each time more aggressively than before. Finally, he grabbed a sheet of paper and jotted down a series of numbers and letters and handed the paper across the counter to Lisa. "There was no exact match for the Patronus Society or Patronus Cult, but there are some matches to Patronus in a few books on religion." He gestured to the sheet of paper. "Those books should help. You'll find them on the second floor." He looked over our heads. "Next."

We were buffeted out of the way by another group of students, so we nervously made our way to the second floor.

I'd heard of the Dewey Decimal System. One of my teachers in elementary school had shown us how to use it to search for stuff. But when we crested the top stair and saw shelf after shelf of books, any knowledge that I might have had tucked away in my head ran screaming from my mind.

Colin gave himself a shake and exhaled a quick breath. "I have an idea. I'll be right back." He sprinted back down the stairs.

"What's he doing?" Lisa asked.

"Who knows?" I looked back at the sea of books. "I don't even know where to start."

"Me neither," Lisa said. "I don't remember the last time I had to look for a book in an actual library. Usually I just open up a browser and *presto*!"

"I know." I looked at the numbers on the sheet and then at the numbers on the shelves. I didn't know if you went right or left or down the rows to another section — or if I was just supposed to close my eyes and click my heels together three times and make a wish.

We were still standing frozen in place when Colin returned.

"Any luck?" he asked.

"Loads," I lied.

"Well, it doesn't matter. Because once again, I have proven just how much of a genius I really am." He slapped a yellow sheet of paper with the back of his hand.

"What's that?" Lisa asked.

He passed the page to her, and she held it up, struggling to read the writing. "What's it say?"

"What do you mean, what's it say?" He snatched the paper back. "It's written in perfect handwriting."

"It looks like a left-handed monkey wrote it," Lisa remarked.

"You just have to squint," Colin said. He held up the paper and cleared his throat. "It says, Professor Meyers, Room 233, Social Sciences Building. Got the info from that creepy librarian."

"I don't get it," I said. "Who's Professor Meyers? And why did the librarian tell you to talk to her?"

Colin smirked. "You know how at school if you ask a teacher a question they always tell you to go look it up?"

Lisa and I nodded.

"Well, the easier way to find the answer is to just ask another teacher."

"I don't get it," I said.

"Look, we can search through these books if you want. But that's going to take us all week. Instead, we could go ask someone who's already read these books." He slapped the paper again. "Professor Meyers."

"I hate to say it," Lisa said, "but from time to time you do make sense, Colin."

"Thank you, Lisa." He smiled. "I wish I could say the same for you."

CHAPTER 21

It took us an hour of walking all over campus before we found the Social Sciences building, and another twenty minutes after that before we found Room 233. Colin stepped boldly to the door and knocked three times.

"Come in," a female voice called from the other side.

Colin opened the door. As soon as we saw Professor Meyers, he and I froze, mouths gaping. Sitting in front of us was the most beautiful woman—like, model-in-a-magazine beautiful—I had ever seen in my life. For some reason, I had expected all professors to be as boring and plain as my parents.

She looked up from her papers when she realized someone was in her office. Her green eyes widened behind her thin, red-framed glasses, and an amused smile flickered at the corners of her lips. "I don't think I have you three in any of my classes," she said. "How can I help you?"

Lisa looked from me and Colin to Professor Meyers and back again. "Oh, you guys are pathetic," she muttered. She turned to Professor Meyers. "I'm Lisa. And these are my friends, Colin and Dean."

"M... my dad works here," I said. "Professor Curse?"

"You're Dean?" She leaned forward in her chair. "The boy who fought off those thieves?"

"I helped fight them too," Colin lied. "There were eight of them. I took out seven and Dean got the eighth." He took a step closer to the teacher. "It was really rough."

Professor Meyers smiled. "I didn't see your name in the paper."

"That's 'cause he wasn't there," Lisa said.

Colin groaned.

"Cute, kid," Professor Meyers said. "Real cute." She turned to Lisa. "What can I do for you guys?"

Lisa smiled. "We're trying to find some information about a secret society, and we were told you'd be the one to ask."

"I do teach a course on secret societies." She brushed a lock of hair out of her face. "Any secret society in particular? There are quite a few, you know."

"The Protection Society," Lisa said.

Professor Meyers squinted and looked off toward the ceiling. "Nope, I've never heard of it."

"You haven't?" I asked. "What about the Patronus Society?"

She smiled. "Ah, you mean the Congregatio de Sacrificio."

"Um... no, I don't think so," I said. "We were told it was called the Patronus Society."

"No doubt from someone who lives in Russia?" she guessed.

"That's right!" Colin exclaimed.

"That's a different name for the Congregatio de Sacrificio." She paused and looked at each of us. "It means the Society of Sacrifice." She leaned toward us a bit more. "The translation was changed a long time ago in Russia to the Protection Society, but I know which group you're talking about. They're incredibly obscure, though. You won't find much information about them."

My words came out in a rush. "Can you tell us what you know?" I gripped the edge of her desk.

She leaned back in her chair in surprise. I imagined her reaching under her desk to press the button for security to have the crazy kid removed from her office. Instead, she nodded. "I like your passion, but let's be clear here, we're talking about something that is generally regarded as a myth. An urban legend. Which is why, I'm afraid, I don't know much. Lots of rumors, mostly." She leaned forward again and looked questioningly at each of us. "I don't get questions about this group from anyone. Not even colleagues. Why are you kids interested?"

I considered lying, but then I remembered that my

dad knew what we were doing here. He didn't think it too strange, plus there was a good chance that Ms. Myers would mention our visit to my dad, so I would be better off telling the truth. Well, half the truth. "I met this guy who's really interested in the group and his interest sort of spurred mine."

"I think it's fascinating," Lisa said. "Who knew there were real secret societies like this?"

Ms. Myers leaned back in her chair and smiled. "I agree, Lisa. One hundred percent. It's refreshing to find youngsters like yourselves who have an interest in the subject. Plus, it's un-common to find people who've even heard about the group, but those who have tend to be very interested. I just wish there was more information."

"We'd appreciate anything you could tell us," Lisa said.

"Well. Let's see." She tapped a delicate finger against the armrest. "Since you spoke to someone who knows the Russian legends, I'll assume you already know that they apparently believed they could stop death."

Colin and I glanced at one another. "Yeah, we heard that. How did they do it?" I asked.

"They didn't *do* it," Professor Meyers said. "They just believed they could."

"Right," Lisa said. "How did they *think* they could?"

"I don't know exactly," she said. "I think it has

something to do with their name. The Society of Sacrifice."

"So you're saying we need to sacrifice a chicken or a pig or something?" Colin asked.

The professor coughed. "W... what?"

"I mean... are you saying that *they* used to sacrifice chickens or pigs?"

"No, I'm not saying that at all." She pursed her lips and raised her eyebrows. She paused, as if she wanted an explanation for what Colin was talking about or maybe just an explanation for Colin in general. When we didn't offer one, she continued. "I'm sure your Russian friend told you about Pripyat, right?"

"Not really," Lisa said. "He mentioned it, but didn't really have time to explain its significance. And we couldn't find anything online about how the town was connected to the society either."

"That's strange." Professor Meyers leaned back and laced her fingers over her stomach. "Hmm, I thought there'd be at least a mention or two online. Pripyat is one of only a handful of references you can find in history books. Any Russian who knows about the society knows about Pripyat."

I felt as if I were at the dentist's office, waiting to find out if they were going to bust out a drill to take care of a cavity. I rubbed the back of my neck. "Can you tell us? Please?"

Professor Meyers gave a thoughtful nod and continued. "Pripyat is a city... village, really... in the Ukraine, not far from Chernobyl." She looked at each of us. "Do you know about Chernobyl?"

I shook my head just as Colin said, "Yeah." He looked at me and Lisa and registered our confusion. "What? You guys don't remember doing a whole unit on Chernobyl in Mrs. Farnsworthy's... " He trailed off as he shivered visibly.

Professor Meyers picked up the story. "In 1986, there was a disaster at the nuclear power plant in Chernobyl."

"That actually does ring a bell," Lisa said.

"Apparently a member of the Congregatio de Sacrificio went to the power plant before the incident and insisted there was going to be some kind of accident. She demanded to speak to the plant foreman."

Colin leaned in. "She knew it was going to explode?"

"It's a story... it's not true." She regarded each of us carefully. "You guys understand that, right?" A moment passed before she continued. "No, the story is that she knew that the two men maintaining the reactor were going to die and that they were going to die together."

"Let me guess," I said. "She told them they had twenty-four hours?"

"That I don't know. But according to what I've heard, she tried everything to stop the two men from going to work. She was convinced she could save them and possibly millions of others."

"Well?" Colin prodded. "Did she do it? Did she save them?"

"Evidently not," Professor Meyers said. "You studied the unit in school, so I'll assume you got to the part where the reactor exploded and millions of people were killed, injured, or poisoned."

"Right," Colin said, "of course. Yeah, I knew that."

"What about the woman?" Lisa asked. "What happened to her?"

"That's where the story ends." Professor Meyers paused again before continuing. "I really need you three to understand that this is myth. There's no real, tangible, firsthand knowledge of this group. What we know comes from rumors, secondhand stories, and conjecture. They... the Congregatio de Sacrificio... appeared to be in the business of preserving life. Some cultural anthropologists have suggested that members of the society were given a gift that helped them know who was in danger. Or that they inherited some kind of warning system that told them when an incident was seconds away from happening."

The visions, I thought. *They're a pretty clear*

warning...

"A gift?" Colin asked. He looked disappointed. "Are you sure it wasn't a curse?"

"Um, well, I don't know how successful a secret society would be if they kept cursing their members. But it is possible."

"How do they get rid of it?" Lisa asked. "The curse... er... I mean the gift."

"From what I gather, they can't. There are rumors that they eventually passed on the gift to someone worthy, moments from death."

"Passed it on? How?" Lisa asked.

"Now that's where the stories tend to differ. I've heard that it's passed with a touch and a single word." She brushed her hands together. "Other accounts say there needs to be blood. I'm sure there's more to it than that. These secret societies tend to have lavish ceremonies for all kinds of things."

My mind flashed to when I had helped Mr. Vidmar. He had grabbed my arm in a vice-like grip. And he had coughed blood all over my Green Day T-shirt. And the word...

"Glimpse," I said, without thinking.

That's when it happened again.

Professor Meyers was leaning forward with a curious expression, and suddenly I had another vision.

The next victim was crouched on top of Professor Meyers's desk. Her face was as twisted as the others— just as horrified and just as desperate. And the scream that came through her lips turned my blood to ice. I recoiled and stumbled against the door. But at least I had the sense to clasp a hand over my mouth to partially stifle my own shriek. Like the others, she was gone as suddenly as she had appeared.

I glanced at the professor—she had recoiled in her chair, her mouth gaped and arms crossed over her chest as if in self-defense. She looked utterly horrified by my display. I lunged for the door and ran down the hall, bursting out of the building and collapsing to my knees on the steps outside.

I glanced at my watch. "Two twenty-three," I muttered to myself, committing the time to memory.

A few second later, Colin and Lisa burst from the building and rushed to my side. "Who... who was it?" Lisa's voice hitched. She and Colin looked equally pale.

"Becky," I said. "It was Becky. My sister's going to die in twenty-four hours."

CHAPTER 22

"She's not going to die," Lisa said. "We're not going to let it happen. We can stop it."

"We can?" Colin asked.

"Yes. We can."

I stopped listening as soon as Lisa and Colin started arguing. My sister's contorted face was seared into my mind. I thought about Mr. Utlet. We had done everything right. We stopped the robbers from killing him, we called the police, we did everything... and for what? He still died. He was still gunned down and not even by the bad guys.

There was something else. That moment just before the police shot him. I closed my eyes to remember. He was standing in the beams of light, and for a fraction of a second, I had imagined what the officers were seeing. I remembered fighting the urge to run out and shield Mr. Utlet from the bullets. And all at once it hit me.

"I was going to die!"

Lisa and Colin stopped shouting at each other and turned toward me slowly. Both of them looked confused and stunned.

"That's why he was in the alley," I said, before they could say a word.

"What are you talking about?" Lisa asked.

"The stopwatches. The ones we saw in the hospital."

"What about them?" Colin prodded.

Lisa gasped. "There was one with your initials on it, wasn't there?"

"Yes," I said. "Colin saw it. Remember?" I looked at Colin, then back to Lisa. "Colin was right."

"I was?" Colin looked even more shocked.

"It was meant for me," I said. "I was supposed to die that day. He saved me. That's why he was in the alley."

"Those guys were going to kill you?" Colin asked. "For what? Your biology textbook?"

"Maybe," I said. "Maybe because I was going to get in the way of their robbery. Or maybe I was going to cut through that alley and get hit by a street-sweeper. Who knows? The point is he intervened somehow, and I'm alive."

"But how would he know your name?" Lisa asked.

"I don't know. Maybe he asked around. Maybe he followed me. Either way, he did."

"Not to be a downer or anything," Colin said, "but it could also be that the initials on the stopwatch were someone else's. Or maybe he started out trying to save people, but eventually he really did go nuts. I mean, you heard Dmitri when he said *suicide*. As in he tried to kill himself."

"Maybe," I conceded. "It's possible that he went nuts. I feel like I'm going nuts every time I see one of these stupid vis—" A shiver rolled up my spine and hitched the words in my throat. "But I think there's something more to this. I really think he saved my life."

"So there's a way," Lisa said before Colin could get in a word. "If you're still alive, then Mr. Vidmar saved your life. And if he could save your life, then we can save Becky's."

We turned to leave, heading in the direction of my father's office, but Colin stopped me by grabbing my arm. He pointed to the corner of the building. "Did you guys see that?"

"See what?" Lisa asked.

"That guy." He took a few cautious steps toward the corner, then peered around the edge. "He's gone." He turned back to us. "You didn't see him?"

"Colin, what are you talking about?" Lisa asked.

"There was someone *there*, watching us, but he took off as soon as I noticed him."

"Wait," I said, remembering the person from the library, "was he wearing a leather jacket?"

"You did see him!"

I shook my head. "No. I thought I saw someone at the library, though."

"You mean you think someone's following us?" Lisa asked. "Who?"

"Oh man," Colin said, "what if it's someone from the cult?"

I considered it for a half a second and then shook my head. "It doesn't matter right now. My sister's going to die, and we can't let that happen. We can worry about who's following us later. Lisa's right. If Mr. Vidmar saved my life, we can save Becky's."

We rushed to my dad's office and told him we were ready to go.

"You got the answers you were looking for?" he asked as we walked to the car.

"Most of them," Lisa said.

My dad started the engine and pulled out of his parking spot. "I want you kids to know that you've made remarkable strides these past few days." He glanced at me. "Going to a funeral, coming to the library to better understand what happened. I'm proud of you." He smiled. "It will get better now, kids. I think after you go to Mr. Utlet's funeral this Saturday you'll see how much better you'll actually feel." He glanced in the rearview mirror and looked at Lisa and Colin. "Do you kids need a ride tomorrow?"

"A ride where, Mr. Curse?" Lisa asked.

"You kids have group therapy tomorrow."

I groaned inwardly. I had forgotten about the sessions—and there was no chance my parents would let me skip the next one. But I had to try.

"Dad, I don't think—"

"We had an agreement, son." My dad's voice was stern, but he was still smiling. "You're going."

Arguing would have been futile. I considered my options. I couldn't pretend to be sick. My parents would see right through it. And even if they did let me stay home, they'd insist I stay in bed. I couldn't help Becky from my bed. I had seen a movie once where a kid put sugar in his parent's gas tank and it stopped the car from working. I considered stuffing my pockets with the tiny packets my parents used in their coffee and quickly wondered how many packets it would take to do the job.

"Your session is at ten, right?" my dad said, glancing at the rearview mirror.

"Er... yes, sir," Lisa said.

"Well, if your parents need me to drive you kids, I'm happy to do it."

"Thanks, sir," Colin said. "I'm sure my parents

would like that. I'll double check."

"Me too," Lisa said.

I shifted in the seat. "How long are the sessions?"

Lisa groaned. "Two hours."

"Unless Eric starts crying again. Last session was almost three hours, thanks to him."

"So we'll be done by noon." I had to be near Becky at 2:23. As early as possible. "What's Becky doing tomorrow?"

My dad cocked an eyebrow. "Becky? She's probably going to spend the day packing. I'm driving her to camp at four."

"So she'll be home the whole morning?"

My dad smiled. "I doubt she'll have plans, son. I'm sure you'll have plenty of time to say goodbye to her after your session."

A knot twisted in my gut. Any other time I'd be all too happy to see Becky leave for a couple weeks. But the thought of saying goodbye to her now, after the way she looked in my vision, was almost too much.

"Easy, champ," my dad said, looking concerned. "She's only going to be gone for two weeks."

"I know that." A drop of water hit my wrist. I rubbed it with my thumb and then wiped my face. Tears? I was *crying*? I used my sleeve and wiped my face again. "I'm not crying," I lied. "I just got some dust in my eye."

"There was a lot of dust in the library," Lisa agreed.

"I didn't think so," Colin said.

"You really don't know when to shut up, do you, Colin?" Lisa muttered, though everyone in the car could hear her.

No way was I getting out of therapy tomorrow. I could take the tires off the car and my dad would strap me to his back and piggyback me to the office. You don't shed tears for a sister going away to bug camp and not get sent to therapy. I was pretty sure there was a rule written in some how-to-be-a-brother handbook that specifically addressed that issue.

CHAPTER 23

I was relieved to find my sister sitting at the kitchen counter with my mom when we got home.

"How'd it go?" Mom asked.

I forced myself to relax. It was surreal to see Becky sitting at the counter. She looked like the picture of health. I shivered. "I think Mr. Vidmar's brother was glad we came. It seemed like he was," I lied.

"I'm sure he was, dear. And how about you? How do you feel?"

"Fine."

My dad leaned over the counter and brought his face to within a few inches of the glass jar in front of Becky. "Another spider? I thought all the bugs had to be different."

"This is not just *another* spider, Dad." Becky scoffed. "This is a *Latrodectus variolus*." She picked up the jar and thrust it toward my dad's face. "Notice the red hourglass on the belly."

"Hourglass? Wait." Dad backed away noticeably. "You mean that's a black widow?"

"It is," Becky said proudly. "And it's my fiftieth specimen, so I have a complete display for camp."

"Aren't those dangerous?" my dad asked.

Becky beamed. "You bet. Its venom is a powerful neurotoxin." She looked over at me. "One bite might not kill an adult, but it would sure do a number on a kid." She tapped the glass. "I'm thinking about training it to attack annoying brothers."

"Wait, it's alive?" I said. "I thought all your bugs were dead and pinned to a board." I narrowed my eyes at the jar and saw the little devil leap onto the side of the glass.

"Well, I had to act quickly to catch this one, and I didn't have time to put it right into a kill jar. Obviously, I need to figure out what the best way to move it is."

"You're going to move it?" I looked at my parents and then back to Becky. "While it's still alive?"

"Dean," my dad said, "if there's anyone who can handle insects, it's your sister. But Becky, when the time comes to move the little sucker, either Mom or I have to be there."

"What!?" I sputtered. This was it. This was how it was going to happen. My sister was going to try to move the spider to her kill jar, and it was going to bite her. That's how she was going to die.

"Thank you, Daddy," Becky said. "But spiders aren't

insects. They're arachnids."

"She's only eleven years old," I said.

"Why do you care anyway?" Becky glared at me from across the counter. "Half of my specimens were poisonous."

"I... I don't care, I just—"

"Dean, it's completely normal for you to suddenly feel overprotective of your family right now," my dad said. "You've been exposed to a series of traumatic incidents, and it's made you hyperaware of threats. This is why it's a good thing you're going to therapy tomorrow."

"Therapy," Becky said with a smirk.

When my dad started talking like a therapist, there was no arguing with him. I pursed my lips and nodded. "You're right," I said. "Sorry, Becky. I'm sure you're going to be careful." I tugged uncomfortably at my tie. "I'm going to go get changed."

I walked up the stairs with one thought. That spider was going to bite Becky. I was sure of it. There was only one solution. It had to die.

Killing the spider posed a bigger problem than I expected. Becky didn't let that stupid jar out of her sight the whole night. She even put it on the table while we ate dinner. I couldn't take my eyes off the eight-legged beast. All I wanted to do was lunge across the table, snatch up the jar, and smash it with a sledgehammer. But every time I thought of doing something to it, I remembered Mr. Utlet and how he had still died even though we intervened. I needed to be careful. The more I thought about it, the more I decided that the only way to protect Becky was to put the spider in a kill jar for her. I shivered at the thought. Why did I have to have a sister with such a stupid hobby?

"So what's in a kill jar anyway?" I asked.

Becky looked up from her plate of fried chicken. "You're actually interested?"

"Just curious," I corrected. My parents looked at me like I was some stranger, so I added, "I'm thinking of making one that's big enough for an eleven-year-old."

"That's not funny, Dean," my mom said.

Becky shoved another chunk of chicken into her mouth. "It's just nail polish remover."

"That's it? Nail polish remover? That's how you kill it?"

"Pretty much. I mean, there's a bit more to it. It's the fumes that actually kill it. But that's mostly it."

Simple enough. Throw some nail polish remover in a jar, toss in the spider, and presto. Dead spider.

"I was going to do it after dinner," she added. "I

guess you can watch if you want."

I opened my mouth to object, but my mom cut me off. "Oh no, you're not, young lady." She picked up the jar and placed it on the ledge behind the sink. "You've killed enough bugs today. The whole place smells like a nail salon. You can do it tomorrow afternoon before we leave—and we'll do it outside."

Becky shrugged. "Okay. It only takes a couple minutes for them to die, and I still need to make the label for it anyway."

I smiled. The knot that had been tightening in my stomach ever since the funeral loosened just a smidgen, and I was able to eat a few bites. I couldn't be one hundred percent sure the black widow would kill Becky, but it made the most sense. And now that Becky would have to wait until tomorrow afternoon to kill the spider, it made even more sense. Two twenty-three. I had until then to get rid of that monstrosity. As soon as Becky went to bed, I'd have my chance. Becky would wake up, happy that she didn't have to do the dirty work, and I would be a bit less anxious about everything. It would all work out.

That was the plan anyway.

CHAPTER 24

It was after midnight when I finally heard my parents go to bed. But I waited another hour before I crept across my room, grabbed the bottle of nail polish remover that I had taken from my mom's bathroom earlier, and inched into the corridor. I could hear my dad's heavy breathing from behind the door at the end of the hall and decided it was safe to proceed. The floor just outside my room groaned under my weight, and I froze, certain someone would wake up and come to investigate. No one did.

I moved down the carpeted staircase and through the living room into the kitchen. Moonlight filtered through the window above the sink and lit up a newly constructed web inside the glass jar. *It's probably asleep. This is going to be easy.* I grabbed a spare jar from under the sink, plucked up the one the black widow called home, and placed them gently on the kitchen counter.

I dumped half the bottle of nail polish remover into the empty jar. The fumes stung my nose and eyes, and I stood back and listened for noises from upstairs. Nothing. *So far so good.* I turned to the jar with the spider and whispered, "Your turn, you little murderer." I twisted the lid but kept it pressed firmly in place. The spider hovered on its web, not moving despite being jostled.

I slowly slid the lid off and turned the jar upside down over the kill jar. I'm not entirely sure if the spider just happened to wake up when I tilted its home, or if it had been lying in wait for me to do something stupid... like remove the lid. I'm thinking it was probably lying in wait. Either way, one second it was perched on a strand of webbing, and the next it was on the edge of the jar, inches from my hand, about to escape. I didn't react at first. I just stood there staring dumbly at the little beast—I imagined it staring back, eyeing me as if it were trying to decide where best to sink its fangs. I could almost see the venom dripping from its mouth. I held my breath, placed the kill jar on the counter, and reached my free hand for the lid so I could at least knock it back into its original jar. But when I moved, the spider moved too.

I panicked and fumbled the jar like some butter-fingered quarterback. It would have crashed to the floor if I hadn't found my grip at the last second. I snatched the lid from the counter and slapped it back into place. I realized two things when I leaned toward the glass jar to make sure I still had the spider trapped. First, I didn't have the spider—the jar was empty—and second, something was tickling the tip of my ear. I jumped and swatted the side of my head like a flea-infested dog, sending the bottle capsized arachnid bouncing across the kitchen table.

A shiver raked up my spine, and I reached for the closest weapon I could find: a fork sitting beside the sink. The spider dodged left, and I lunged. The metal prongs found their mark, impaling the spider's bulbous backside and pinning it to the counter. It twitched twice and then stopped.

Interesting fact: spiders don't go limp when they die. They look pretty much exactly the same as they do when they're alive. So I stood there for a few minutes, half expecting the widow to somehow dislodge the fork from the table and walk away. When I was sure it was dead, I picked up the spider with the fork, used the lip of the jar to pull the monster off, and then replaced the lid. I wiped up the mess I'd made, poured the nail polish remover back into the bottle, and cleaned up the kill jar, which I hadn't needed after all. When I was finished, I returned the jar with the spider-corpse to the ledge behind the sink.

Hopefully, Becky wouldn't see the fork holes. If she did, I thought I could convince her that they'd always been there. Who knows? Maybe some species of spider breathe through their backs like whales or dolphins.

When I was confident the kitchen was in pretty

much the same state I had found it in, I snuck back to my room and crawled into bed. Even though it felt as though spiders were crawling all over me, I felt pretty good about myself. The whole kill-the-spider thing hadn't gone entirely as planned, but I'd successfully saved my sister's life. Not that she would ever know it. Just to be safe, I'd stick to her side like a fat kid on a cookie, at least until 2:23. But she definitely would *not* have a death by spider bite.

I closed my eyes and drifted off.

I woke up to a shriek rattling the rafters.

CHAPTER 25

I knew the difference between a scared shriek and an angry one, and the one that had woken me definitely sounded angry. Still, my heart was pounding as I rushed downstairs. When I ran to the kitchen and saw Becky, flanked by Mom and Dad, gaping at the dead spider in Becky's palm, I wished I had taken my time.

"*He* did it!" Becky's pale finger pointed at me. "I know he did!"

"Dean?" my dad said, repositioning the glasses on the bridge of his nose. "Do you have any idea how Becky's spider was... er—"

"Murdered!" Becky seethed.

I reviewed the scene calmly. Dad looked at ease, Mom looked horrified, and Becky looked as though she were about to blow up. My eyes landed on the spider sitting on Becky's palm. The holes on its back glared accusingly.

There was no point lying. "Look," I said. "I was trying to help."

"See!" Becky jumped up from the table. "I told you

he did it."

"I didn't want you to get bitten, so I tried to make that kill jar thing."

"You tried to make a kill jar?" Her free hand balled into a fist at her side. "With what? Nails? Argh." She grabbed a small jar from the counter and shoved it in my face. A wad of cotton sat on the bottom and a disk of cardboard hovered midway, dividing the jar in half. "This is a kill jar! This! You soak the cotton, divide the jar, and the fumes kill the bug. The fumes!" She pointed at me again. "You did it on purpose. You knew I needed fifty specimens, and you made it so I can't use this one."

"Why can't you use it?" I asked. "Can't you just pin it to the board like that?"

Becky put one hand on her hip. "Hmmm, Ms. Curse," she squeaked, "you have an interesting specimen. May I ask what method you used to kill it?" She shifted her hands so they were clasped innocently at her waist. "Oh, sure, Mrs. Randson, well, for most of them I used a kill jar, but for that one, I decided that a nail was the best way to go."

"It was a fork," I corrected.

"A fork!" She looked at my dad. "He stabbed my spider with a fork! Tell me that's enough to have him committed." She looked back at me. "You're sick, you know that? Really sick."

I shrugged helplessly. "It was about to get away." I looked at my parents. My mom's mouth was hanging open so low I swear the spider would have fit inside easily. But my dad looked as unsurprised as before. "It's not uncommon for kids to take out their aggression on animals or insects, Dean. But it really isn't the best way to deal with the emotions you're having. And it's certainly not fair to the animal."

"I didn't *want* to stab it," I protested. "It was going to escape and probably kill someone. I had to stop it from getting away." I rolled my eyes and looked up at the ceiling. "It's just a stupid spider. Jeez."

"It's nine, Dean," my dad said, pointing to the clock. "You should get ready. We don't want to be late for your session."

"I don't need therapy, Dad. I really think it would be best if I just stayed home today."

Dad raised an eyebrow. He wasn't buying it. I wondered if I should just tell him. Come clean and everything. He might believe me if I kept it straight to the point: *Dad, I am having visions of people twenty-four hours before they die.*

It only took me a second to imagine that conversation and another second to imagine the scene that would follow while he chased me around the house with restraints. And I would be no good to Becky locked up in the loony bin. Honesty was the best policy most of the time, but not all the time. Not now.

My dad cleared his throat. "I suspect you'll find it a slightly better outlet for your feelings than forking spiders in the middle of the night, son." I opened my mouth to explain again that it hadn't been my plan to stab the spider, but he held up his hand. "Get ready. We'll leave in half an hour."

A circle of chairs greeted Colin, Lisa, and me when we walked into the counseling room. Eric Feldman sat beside Rodney and three other kids I knew from school. Eric's head was bowed and he had his arms folded across his chest. Rodney was doing the same. I had a pretty good idea why they were here: fake how badly they were handling the incident, and score some sympathy. It's not like either of them had witnessed their neighbor get shot by the police or gotten caught in some back alley fight. I wanted to kick them both in the head. The others were chattering away to each other as if they were at the mall rather than at grief therapy.

The doctor stood up to greet us when we walked in. He was a rail of a man with thin gray hair and an unnaturally dark beard that made him look as though he actually dyed his facial hair rather than the hair on his head.

"Dean? I'm Dr. Mickelsen." He extended his hand. "I'm glad you decided to join us today. I've spoken with your dad, and he's given me a bit of information about how you're doing."

"Thank you, sir," I said, shaking his hand. Nerves twisted my stomach. "Um... when did you talk to my dad?"

If my dad had talked to him yesterday, then Dr. Mickelsen would assume I was just some poor kid who had seen more than my fair share of trauma this past week. But if Dad talked to him this morning, the doctor would know about the whole spider incident and think I was some nutcase who went around stabbing insects with forks.

"I just talked to him this morning." He smiled and gestured to the chairs. "Shall we begin?

This morning? Great. He thinks I'm nuts.

When we took our chairs, Dr. Mickelsen plopped back into his, opened up a leather-bound notepad, and then looked around expectantly.

"Who'd like to begin?" he said. Without pausing, he turned to me. "Dean? How about you? Since this is your first session, perhaps you could introduce yourself and maybe tell us just a bit about how you're feeling."

I knew everyone in the circle. Lisa and Colin were on

my right. Eric Feldman and a couple of his loser followers were on my left. I didn't really see how introducing myself was going to be helpful. I glanced at my watch. It was already after ten, and all I could think about was Becky. Was she okay? Did she catch another spider, something even more dangerous than her stupid black widow?

Is there something worse than a black widow?

"Dean?"

"Oh, right, sorry." I took a breath. "I'm Dean Curse. I... um... I know everyone in this circle, and I'm feeling a bit, well, confused. Thank you."

"Thank you for that introduction, Dean. I think you'll find that confusion is a fairly common emotion for people who have experienced what you have gone through." His gaze tracked around the group. "Anyone else?"

Eric put up his hand.

"Oh, brother," Colin muttered. "Here we go."

"Mr. Blane," the shrink said, pointing his mechanical pencil at Colin. "Rule number one in this circle is trust. Trust that this is a judgment-free zone, and that anything you say or do here is free from ridicule."

Colin rolled his eyes. "Sorry, sir."

"Go ahead, Eric," Dr. Mickelsen said.

"I don't just feel confused. I feel really, really angry." There were no tears, but Eric swiped the sleeve of his shirt across his face anyway. He went on for another fifteen minutes about how traumatized he was from the accident. He finished his little sob-fest with, "Why did this have to happen to one of the nicest teachers at school?"

I didn't mean to, but a laugh escaped my lips. It was just so pathetic the way he was going on.

Eric turned in his seat and glared. All traces of sorrow evaporated. "Something funny, Curse?"

"Why are you even here, Eric? You weren't near the explosion and you didn't even like Mrs. Farnsworthy."

"That's not true!" Eric leaned forward. "She was my favorite teacher." He turned back to the doctor. "I'm angry that something this terrible happened to her. She was so kind."

"Oh, please," I mumbled to myself. I shook my head and turned back to Dr. Mickelsen. He looked at me, at Eric, and then scribbled something on the pad.

"You bring up an excellent point, Eric." He leaned forward in his chair. "Actually, anger is the topic I wanted us to focus on today. It's entirely normal for people to have feelings of rage when they experience traumatic events." He looked around the group. "Some people direct their anger toward other people, some go and vandalize property, and others... " His gaze landed on me and stopped. "Others take their rage out on animals."

"Animals?" Lisa looked disgusted.

Colin glanced between me and Dr. Mickelsen and whispered, "Why's he looking at you?"

"Does anyone else have any problems with anger?" He quickly looked around the group and paused on Rodney for a moment before settling on me again. "Dean? How about you?"

I shook my head. "Nope. I'm not angry." If there was one thing I had learned from my dad, it was that counseling sessions ended early when no one shared their feelings and lasted hours when people did. I glanced at my watch. 11:23. I hated that I couldn't be near Becky right now. If the spider wasn't the cause of her death, I only had a few hours to help her.

"Animals can seem easy targets," the doctor continued. "But to hurt one, or kill one—"

"Are you suggesting someone here killed an animal? Because they were angry?" Lisa leaned forward and scowled around the circle. "Who?"

Eric pointed at me. "Dean's the one who looks the angriest. I bet he did it."

"I'm not angry," I growled.

"Dean wouldn't do that," Lisa added. She looked at me. "Right?"

I gave my head a quick shake.

Eric stood up and took a couple steps across the

circle toward me. "Obviously you did it. We can all see the way the doctor is looking at you."

"Eric," Dr. Mickelsen said. "I think it's best if you take your—"

"What?" Eric added, leaning over me. "You're so tough you have to kill little puppies?"

"Puppies?" Lisa's eyes widened to the size of lightbulbs.

"I didn't kill any puppies," I said. I felt my face flush. "And I'm not angry." My hands started shaking, and I felt rage building inside me. Not just toward Eric, but toward the entire situation. My sister could very well be lying in a ditch someplace bleeding to death. I needed to be with her, not here.

"Yeah, that's why you look so scared." He poked me in the chest. "You know who the kindest and most gentle person I knew was?" Eric added. "Mrs. Farnsworthy."

"Mr. Feldman," the doctor said sternly. "Please take your seat so we can cont—"

"She wouldn't hurt a fly," Eric added. He reached out and poked me again. "You're sick, Curse. You're really si—"

I don't really remember jumping up, and I don't really remember my fist connecting with the side of Eric's face. But that's exactly what happened. One second he was leaning over me, and the next he was lying on his back on the ground and I was staring down at him, stunned. The circle grew by at least a foot as everyone pushed back their chairs. Except for Colin. He stood up and started clapping as though he'd just seen the final act of an award-winning play.

The doctor was on his feet too, but he wasn't clapping. He glanced from Eric to me and then back to Colin. "Take your seat, Colin," he said finally. "And Dean, I need you—"

"I'm not angry!" I jerked my head from one person to the next. "It was a spider." I looked at Lisa. "My sister had a black widow that escaped from the jar. That's what I stabbed."

"You stabbed a spider?" Lisa asked.

"A poisonous spider," I said. "One that can *kill*."

"You stabbed it?" Colin dropped back into his chair and clapped his hands together, looking far too impressed. "Awesome."

"It was late," I said desperately, my eyes on Lisa. "I couldn't get it into the kill jar. And the first thing I grabbed was a fork."

I heard scribbling behind my shoulder and turned to see that Dr. Mickelsen had taken his seat again and was jotting down notes at blinding speed.

"Thank you for sharing, Dean," he said. "So if I understand you correctly," he looked down at his notes, "you got up in the middle of the night, tried to force a spider into what you call a *kill jar*, and when it wouldn't do as you wanted, you stabbed it with a... um... " His fingers traced the words. "Oh, yes. You stabbed it with a fork." He looked up from his notepad. "Do I have that right?"

I glared at Dr. Mickelsen. I was tired of trying to defend myself, and what was the point anyway? My behavior lately had been too erratic, too suspicious not to cause alarm. If I were a psychologist, I would think I was nuts too.

I knew what I was about to do next would only convince my father that I needed to be committed. The best way to get him off my back was to make it through this session without any more incidents.

But I could only think of my sister. I could only think of how I had failed with Mr. Utlet—I wasn't going to fail with Becky too.

I gave my chair a kick. It skidded out of the way, and I bolted for the door. The last thing I saw as I ran out was Dr. Mickelsen's surprised but strangely satisfied expression as he jotted down even more notes.

CHAPTER 26

I burst through the door at full speed, raced down the corridor, and rushed out of the building. It wasn't until I stopped to get my bearings and let my eyes adjust to the light that I realized Lisa and Colin were right behind me.

"We figured you might need some company in whichever insane asylum they decide to send you to," Colin said.

"Thanks, guys," I managed. I glanced around the mostly deserted parking lot and considered our options. We were downtown. I'd never walked home from this far away, and I couldn't work out how long it would take us to get there if we ran—more time than we had, I figured.

Lisa seemed to be thinking the same thing, and after a couple seconds she gestured to the left. "We run to the mall and catch a bus. We'll be back at your place just afternoon."

We took off, racing across parking lots, cutting through yards, hopping fences, and ducking down alleys. The only time we slowed down was when we hit an intersection that was too busy to rush through. We

191

made it to our stop just as the bus was shutting its doors. Lisa slammed on the glass until the grumbling driver let us in.

For twenty-five minutes, I didn't move a muscle, except for the trembles I couldn't control.

I burst into the kitchen and startled Mom as she was wiping down the counter.

"Good God, Dean, you scared me," she said. She fanned herself with the washcloth and then added, "What happened? The therapist just called and said you three—"

"Where's Becky?" I asked, cutting my mom off and glancing in the living room.

"She's off looking for another insect for her collection."

"She's what!? You told me that she was staying home all day! *You* said she had too much packing to do and that she wasn't going to leave the house."

Mom frowned at my tone. "It's important to her, Dean." She folded the dish towel and hung it on the handle to the oven. "She took her net to the park. I'm sure she'll be back before—"

I spun toward the backdoor and sprinted out of the

house. Lisa and Colin were right behind me. The park was only three blocks away, but I knew it would be packed with people during the summer holidays and with such perfect weather. I glanced at my watch.

"It's 12:25," I huffed. "We don't have much time."

As expected, the park was crowded. I shielded my eyes from the sun and tried to spot my sister. "We have to split up," I said. "Lisa, you have the phone. If we don't find her by two, call 911 and tell them there's been an accident at the park." She nodded. "She's looking for bugs, guys. She'll have her net. Look for a girl with a net."

Colin was too out of breath to speak, but he nodded his head and jogged off to the right. Lisa went left, and I headed straight for the creek.

"Becky!" I called as I ran around the park. I probably circled it at least a dozen times, shouting at girls who looked like Becky, only to find out they weren't her. I checked the whole length of the creek and all the bushes. I ran into Colin and Lisa twice while we were doing our laps. They were having as little luck as I was.

By 2:15, my whole body was trembling. I looked to

my left and saw a hill that might give me a better view of the park and sprinted to the top. A man and woman were filming the view with a small handheld video camera.

"Becky!" I called again.

The man must have heard the desperation in my voice and turned to me. "Did you lose someone, kid?"

"My sister," I said without looking up. I didn't dare stop scanning the park.

"What does she look like?" the woman asked, suddenly by my side.

"S... she's eleven," I said. "She has frizzy hair, and she'll be holding a bug-catching net."

"There's a girl with a net," the man said, pointing off in the distance.

I peered toward where he had indicated, but saw nothing.

"There, kid. Right there." He crouched slightly so his head was at the same level as mine. And then I saw her. I had never been happier to see Becky's frizzy head. She was swinging her net through the air, following an insect that was flying just out of her reach. She was moving back and forth, headed straight for the street. My gaze shifted to the end of the road just as a black BMW squealed around the corner. Like I had with Mr. Utlet, I saw what was going to happen. This time, though, I sprang forward even as the colors around the park drained away, leaving the once bright scene tombstone gray.

My legs burned but didn't slow. I wanted to scream and warn Becky to stop chasing that stupid bug, but if I shouted I'd have to slow down to catch my breath. I could run or scream, but not both. As I moved closer, I saw the guy driving the car that was hurtling toward my sister. He was fiddling with something, his attention split between the road and whatever was on the seat beside him. I wasn't going to make it; there was no way. Becky was at the far end of the park and the BMW was going to pass me any second.

Suddenly it made sense. Mr. Vidmar's hospital visits, his stints in the psych wards... people thought he was trying to kill himself, but he wasn't. He was trying to save people. *The Society of Sacrifice*. People who sacrificed themselves for others. Mr. Vidmar wasn't just trying to save the people in his visions. He put his life in jeopardy to save them. When he jumped off bridges, got electrocuted, and fought off criminals, he was doing that to save lives. He put his life in jeopardy to save *me*. And the color fading away moments before Mr. Utlet died— moments before my sister might die—was a warning... A warning telling me to act.

I knew what I had to do. I veered toward the street and forced myself to move faster, even though every muscle in my body burned with exhaustion. The engine of the car revved, growling like a monster. I was only a couple feet ahead of the car when I hit the curb. Color rushed back a second before I took a deep breath, closed my eyes, and jumped.

CHAPTER 27

The sharp fumes of cleaning solvent burned my lungs every time I breathed in. I opened my eyes. I found myself staring at an oversized fluorescent light. I blinked twice, and a sudden rush of pain spread over my body. And then I remembered: the screech of rubber on concrete and, a moment later, the car slamming into my side. *Becky!* I tried to shift my body but couldn't.

"He's awake." Lisa stepped up to the edge of my bed, leaned down, and gave me a quick hug. Then she whispered in my ear, "Becky's fine."

A wave of relief washed over my body, temporarily numbing the pain. I had done it. I had saved my sister!

My mom was suddenly at my side. Her eyes were red and puffy. "What were you thinking?"

My excitement began to fade when I saw her worn face. "W... what happened?"

"What happened is you ran across the street without looking, young man." My dad's stern voice came from the front of the room. When I lifted my head, I realized that one of my legs was partially suspended off the bed, covered in a white cast. Tubes and wires from half a dozen machines connected to various parts of my body hummed and whirred as they delivered fluids and monitored my system. I groaned.

"Lisa, honey," my dad said. "Would you please go to the nurses' station and let them know that Dean's awake. See if they can give him something for the pain." He looked back at me. "We can talk about how you forgot the whole look-both-ways-before-you-cross bit later." He stood up and took a deep breath. "Unless you have something to say for yourself right now."

As I registered the suspicion in my father's voice, I realized what was going through his head. He thought I jumped in front of the car to kill myself! *Well, technically, Dean, that's exactly what you did.*

"Nah," I said finally. "There's really nothing to say. I was just running to catch up to my friends and forgot to look."

Dad nodded slowly. "Well, remember our deal, Dean. Be honest about everything, right?"

"I am, Dad." But I knew I could never tell my dad the truth. He'd stay cool on the outside, but he'd bring home a straitjacket and lock me in the basement if I told him I had visions of people dying.

"All right." Dad exchanged a look with my mother. "All right, well, what matters is that you are fine, except for a few broken bones. Do you want me to sit you up a bit?"

"Yeah, thanks."

"Be careful," Mom said. She turned her watery eyes to me. "You broke your leg, three ribs," tears started tracking down her cheeks, "and your wrist."

"That explains the pain," I said, forcing a smile that only made my mom's tears flow faster. "I'm fine, Mom, I'll heal. Don't worry."

"Well, I'm glad you're fine, you jerk!" Becky's snarling face came into view as my dad raised the head of the bed. "I should be at entomology camp right now, but instead I have to visit my stupid, bug-killing brother in the hospital."

"We said we'd take you today," my dad said. "The camp is two weeks long. I'm sure you won't miss much. And I think your being here is more important. Don't you?"

Becky growled and stormed out of sight.

"I'm sorry she's missing her camp," I said. "You guys should take her now."

Dad shook his head. "I think you'll find that your sister is more upset that you're injured than she is about missing a day or two of camp. She just isn't ready to show that yet. But we're going to take her as soon as you get something for the pain."

As if on cue, Lisa strolled back in, followed by a

short nurse in bright yellow scrubs. She jotted down some numbers on a chart and injected the contents of a large syringe into the tube that ran to my arm. Almost instantly, a warm numbness spread through my body.

"I think I should stay here," my mom said.

"No, no, it's fine, Mom. You should go. Lisa and Colin will keep me company." My mom opened her mouth to protest, but I added, "I'm fine. Honest. I think Becky would want both of you to drop her off. It is just two weeks after all."

"Yeah, Mrs. Curse, we'll keep him company," Lisa said.

"Where is Colin, anyway?" I asked.

"We were going to get you flowers," Lisa said, "but Colin said you'd appreciate hot dogs a lot more."

Usually he'd be right, but I felt too weak to even stomach the idea of them.

"You're sure you'll be okay?" my mom asked.

I nodded.

"Okay." She wiped her face with a Kleenex. "It's only a couple hours' drive. We'll be back before dinner."

My dad clapped his hands. "All right then. I'll go pull the car around."

"I'll just check in with the doctor one more time before we go," my mom said. "But I'll grab Becky and meet you outside."

Dad nodded. "We'll see you in a few hours, champ."

As soon as my parents left—Mom hovered a bit longer—I heard a knock at the door. "Can I come in?" I recognized the Russian accent even before I saw the familiar leather jacket. I frowned, feeling as if I had forgotten something.

"Dmitri?"

He winced when he saw my injuries. "You don't look good."

I looked at Lisa, but she looked as confused as I was. "W... what are you doing here?" I asked.

"I'm sorry about the other day. About chasing you out of the church. Ever since I've been thinking... what if you three weren't just pulling my leg? What if you weren't working with that cult? And even if you were, what if you could lead me to them? I... I've been following you since you came by."

"That was you at the library?" I asked. That was what I was supposed to remember—the leather jacket! "And at the university?"

He nodded. "I'm sorry for the things I said to you and your friends, Dean. But you have to understand, I just lost my brother. And I used to see my brother in the hospital more than I saw him out of it."

I decided not to tell him that we'd already seen Mr. Vidmar's chart. Instead, I just nodded.

"When you were asking me questions at the church, I saw something in your face. Something I recognized."

"You did?"

"My brother went to Pripyat and came back different, Dean. At first he was scared all the time. Just the way you were when I saw you. And now"—he waved his hand at the riggings and machines around my bed—"you're in a hospital, lucky to be alive, and yet you don't look the slightest bit scared. That's how my brother always looked when I'd visit him too. So calm, even though half his bones were broken."

He walked over to the television mounted on the wall and pivoted it so it pointed at the bed. "So yesterday, when I followed you, imagine my surprise when I saw what happened." He pulled out a small camcorder from the pocket of his jacket and a wire from the other. "Does this look familiar?" He held up the silver video camera. I shook my head. "On the hill. In the park? You don't remember the man who was filming up there?"

"Y... yeah, I remember." Worry the size of a tennis ball lodged in my throat. I looked at Lisa. Her mouth had dropped open, and she was staring at Dmitri with wide, terrified eyes.

"He filmed the whole thing, Dean." Dmitri plugged one end of the cable into the camera and the other into the back of the TV. "He kept filming as you were running and kept filming after you ran out to the street. Or"—he paused and looked over at me—"as you jumped in front of that car."

"I just—"

Dmitri held up his hand. "He wanted to give the footage to reporters," he continued. "I guess a story about some crazy, suicidal kid sells." He fiddled with the wires. "After what you did for my brother, I decided to return the favor and... I... er... convinced him to give me the camera." He pushed a few buttons and the screen flashed to the scene at the park. "I want to show you something." He pointed to the lower corner of the screen. "See this little girl with a bug net? That's your sister." He eyed me with a cocked eyebrow. "But you already know that."

The scene played out on the twenty-one-inch screen. I watched myself run down the hill. Dmitri paused the film when I was halfway across the soccer pitch. "Here's the thing, Dean. Up to this point you're running like a madman straight toward your sister. She's the one you're trying to get to. But right here, right before you change direction, I think you realized something." He tapped the black BMW. "You realized that your sister was going to step onto the street, with the car headed straight for her. And you realized you couldn't get to her in time, didn't you?" He pressed PLAY again without waiting for me to answer.

"There you go—you've changed direction. Now watch this. This is actually pretty amazing." Onscreen, I was running straight for the street. I swallowed, knowing what was about to happen. "Ready," Dmitri said. "Here." He paused the screen again just as I took off from the curb. "You are jumping like an Olympic track star, Dean. And you did it to save your sister. Didn't you?"

He flicked off the screen and unhooked the camcorder before turning back to me. He walked to the foot of my bed and brushed a lock of hair out of his eyes, then folded his arms across his chest and waited. His rigid stance and narrowed stare made it clear that he wasn't going to leave without an answer.

"Yes," I said.

"My brother... " He took a deep breath and looked up at the ceiling and then back at me. "My brother wasn't crazy, was he?"

"I don't think so, sir," I said.

"And all the times the hospital said that he tried to kill himself? That was... ?"

"I think... I think every time he was in the hospital it was because he got hurt saving someone else. He was pretty much the bravest man I've ever met."

Dmitri swiped a hand across his eyes and looked away.

"I didn't save your brother," I added. "He was there in the alley because of me. He was there to save me. My initials were on the back of one of his stopwatches."

Dmitri nodded and squeezed the bridge of his nose. "Thanks, kid." He cleared his throat. "Thanks a lot. But I don't want what happened to my brother to happen to you. I'll go back to Russia and I'll track down members of that group. There has to be a way to... get rid of whatever this is."

I drew a deep breath and smiled. "Actually, sir, I think I'll keep it."

"What?" Dmitri looked shocked. "But you almost died."

Lisa put her hand on my shoulder. It felt like a sign of support, so that's how I took it. She smiled, and I turned back to Dmitri.

"I saved my sister, sir. If I didn't have this... whatever this is... she'd be dead. In fact, I think Lisa was right all along—this isn't a curse at all."

Dmitri smiled. "You remind me of my brother." He snatched up a pen from the table beside the bed and wrote his phone number on my casted leg. "If you need anything, any time, just call." He patted my foot and left the room without another word.

"Wow," Lisa said. "When you see it played out like that, it really is pretty amazing what you—" A rustle made Lisa stop talking. "I think there's someone in your bathroom," she whispered.

I shifted as best I could and watched Becky come into view through the open bathroom door. She would've been able to hear everything Dmitri had said and watch the whole thing play out on the TV screen. She walked over to my bed and stared down at me. She swallowed and then lowered her head to my chest and wrapped her arms around me. "Thank you," she whispered.

"Dean, have you seen your sis—" my mom said from the doorway. "Oh... um... is everything okay?"

Becky straightened and wiped her sleeve across her eyes. "Yeah, Mom, everything's fine. I'm ready to go."

"Have fun at bug camp, you nerd," I teased.

She smiled and nudged my shoulder. "See you in a couple weeks, loser."

Mom watched, mesmerized, as Becky left. Clearly, she couldn't wrap her head around Becky and me being nice to one another. She walked over, planted a kiss on my forehead, and then left the room. Colin entered just as she left, carrying three tinfoil-wrapped hot dogs. He caught Lisa wiping her cheeks.

"Oh man, Lisa, he's fine. Stop your blubbering."

She ignored him. "What now, Dean?" she asked.

"What do you mean?"

"I mean, what are you going to do about your

visions? If you keep having them... ?"

Colin answered before I had a chance. "If he does, we really need to figure out a better way of dealing with them. This whole jumping in front of moving vehicles is going to get old real fast."

"I second that," I said. "Now give me one of those hot dogs. I think my appetite's back—I'm starving."

Lisa laughed and poked one of the IV bags by my bed. "I have a feeling we're going to have a very strange summer."

I was released from the hospital after three days. Hospitals tend to smell a lot like diapers and beef soup—a combination I couldn't easily get used to—so I was happy to leave. I think the nurses and doctors were even happier to see me go. Getting me out of there meant they got rid of Colin too. The last time he visited, he spent an hour testing how many wooden tongue depressors he could fit in his mouth (fifty-six, in case you were wondering).

It felt wonderful to be back in my own bed, among my own things. I settled in, thinking everything was perfect, until I reached my good arm toward the stack of comic books and noticed a piece of parchment, folded in half and resting on top of my reading material. My name was written in perfect cursive across the front.

My breath hitched when I unfolded the letter.

Dear Dean,
Welcome to the club. We'll be in touch.
C.S.

The initials were like two cymbals clanging in my head. I didn't know what was going to happen next, but I knew darn well who C.S. was: *the Congregatio de Sacrificio.*

The visions continue... in the second book of
THE DEAN CURSE CHRONICLES

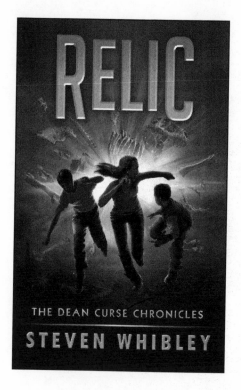

I still wouldn't call it a *gift*. I mean, who wants to have visions of people twenty-four hours before they die? But I suppose it's not a curse either. The problem is, once you have the vision, you *have* to act. You can't just ignore it. If you do, someone's going to die, and like it or not, you'd be at least partially responsible. So my friends and I made a decision. We'll do what it takes to save anyone we can. If that means fighting a monk, stealing back a severed head, or destroying a sixty-five million year old T-Rex, so be it.

ISBN 978-0-9919208-4-6 / PB
ISBN 978-0-9919208-5-3 / HC

Coming in July 2013

THE DEAN CURSE CHRONICLES

STEVEN WHIBLEY

Q & A WITH STEVEN WHIBLEY

Where did the idea for the Dean Curse Chronicles come from?

Most of my book ideas start with a daydream—or night-dream I suppose. Usually I'll just see a scene play out, and my mind will run with it. The **Dean Curse Chronicles** was no exception, and I distinctly remember it.

There was a boy, about 13 or 14 years old, sitting in history class while his teacher droned on about the War of 1812. He was only half paying attention when suddenly his teacher was beside him... only not really, because she was still at the front of the class too. He straightened up and blinked at the new teacher, and then glanced at the teacher at the front of the room, then back to the new teacher, then over his shoulder at his best friend sitting behind him, who, it seemed, hadn't noticed the arrival of the peculiar twin.

The twin-teacher slowly began to shift... She dropped a shoulder and twisted her waist. Then she hunched forward, and her right arm stiffened and twisted upward. Her face became the color of wet clay, and her mouth slowly opened until she resembled a crumpled, zombie-like version of herself.

Then she screamed.

It was a terrifying shrill cry that sent the already horrified kid to the ground. And, just like that, it was over. The kid was on the ground, panting and sweating, but the twisted version of his teacher was gone. More than that, it was clear he'd been the only one to notice the apparition.

My daydream ended, and I just knew the teacher had 24 hours to live and the boy was the only one who could save her.

Only... if you've read the story, you know that Dean had a bit of a learning curve to overcome when it came to saving people.

How did you come up with the name Dean Curse for the main character?

I have a brother named Dean, and most people who know me think I based the character off him. The truth is, I'm a fan of the show *Supernatural*, and an image of the main character popped into my head when I was searching for a first name. As any fan of the show will tell you, the main characters on the show are Sam and Dean Winchester. The "Curse" part of the name happened quite by accident. I was scrambling to write out the scene I'd just daydreamed, and I had the idea to name the kid Dean Cruise, but when I typed it, my fingers typed Dean Curse, and I stopped. Another scene played out in my head: it was the kid addressing the reader at the start of the book. "My name's Dean. Dean Curse. Yes, I see the irony in my name, no need to mention it..." and that made me smile. So I went with it.

How many books are there going to be in the Dean Curse Chronicles?

Well, since I'm putting these books out on my own, that depends in large part on the readers. For now there will be three, but I have ideas for so many more. One of my favorite book series as a kid was *The Hardy Boys*. I liked that there was a definite story line that encompassed the series, but at the same time, each book was its own mystery. I wanted to do something similar with Dean Curse.

Do you have a favorite character?

Becky, Dean's little sister. I don't know why, but she really reminds me of my sisters (I have four). Not that any of my sisters have crazy hair or really bizarre hobbies. There is something nostalgic about the dynamic between Dean and Becky, and I really enjoy writing scenes where they're interacting.

A close second, however, is Mr. Woodward. I based him loosely on a teacher I had in high school who was, hands down, my favorite teacher from any year in any school. He was a guy you knew had lived a crazy, interesting life just by looking at him, but his stories were just too crazy to be real... only they were real. I still smile when I think about some of his classes.

How long did it take you to write the first book?

About a month and a half, but I have a bit of a process when I write a book, and part of that process is putting the book in a "drawer" for a few weeks and then doing a rewrite. So from the time I started writing until the time it was ready to go to an editor, it was about three and a half months.

The cover art is incredible. Who is the artist?

To say I got lucky with the cover designer would be a gargantuan understatement. The artist is Pintado, and to those interested in discussing a project can reach him at rogerdespi.8229@gmail.com. He was a dream to work with, and he paints like a boss!

Did you always want to be a writer?

No. I was always a reader, and in university, I did best in the classes that assigned lots of papers. But writing— especially writing fiction—wasn't even on my radar. I always imagined I'd be a firefighter like my dad or maybe a paramedic. It wasn't until I really fell in love with traveling that I started having these book ideas roll around my mind. And it wasn't until my late-twenties, while I was working in the trades, that I was temporarily injured and wasn't able to work for a while that I decided to try to write something.

Was *Glimpse*, the first book in the Dean Curse Chronicles, your first completed project?

No, *Glimpse*, book one in the series, was my fourth book. My first few manuscripts were not very good and have been bound and gagged and locked forever in a trunk marked SHAME. If any of them try to escape, I will hunt them down and kill them.

How long did it take you to get an agent or publisher interested in your work?

It was years—and many failed manuscripts—before I finally wrote something that caught the attention of agents and publishers. I am presently represented by Jim McCarthy at Dystel Goderich Literary Management, and I couldn't be more pleased. They have a great team set up over there, and they really look out for an author's best interests.

On your blog, you mention that you hate monkeys. Is that really true?

In my experience, the people who love monkeys are people who have never interacted with a monkey in the wild. They've only seen them in zoos where they might do cute things like blow kisses or steal hats from unsuspecting visitors. They've never stared down a charging monkey (or many charging monkeys). They've never had a troop of monkeys descend on them like a gang of hoodlums and literally mug them of all their belongings. Because, if they had, they'd know that monkeys are terrifying creatures with teeth like daggers, and they work in teams. The only defense I've found effective is weeping like a little girl. For some reason monkeys don't kill grown men who weep like 6 year olds. Oh, and if you fancy trying your luck with a mob of monkeys, I suggest taking a trip to Indonesia.

What was your first real job?

I had a paper route that I did for a summer. I also used to wander house to house after it snowed and offer to clear driveways, but that was all in elementary school, so I won't count those. My first real job was a gas station attendant. I was in grade ten, and I used to ride my bike to work after school. It was great because the station was in such a bad location that it got almost no business. I used to do my homework then sit and read novels for hours. Sometimes I'd offer to do double shifts just because it was so easy. As you might have guessed, the station eventually went under, and I took a position at another station, which wasn't nearly so slow, and I didn't get any time to do my homework.

What is your favorite memory as a kid?

Hmm, that's tough. I had a great childhood. I had great friends who I used to get into trouble with, and we lived in a town full of parks and forests and beaches and just all kinds of places to explore. But, if I had to pick one memory, it would be chasing headless chickens... Oh, you want more information about that? We had a small farm when I was growing up, and one of the things we did was butcher our own chickens. It sounds horrifying now, but my dad and older brothers would lop the heads off the chickens, and then they'd drop them, and those chickens would run. My little sisters and I would try to catch them.

When I read that back, it sounds like I grew up in a very disturbing environment, but it doesn't feel like it.

What was your best subject in school?

The only two classes I ever got an "A" in were Japanese and Physical Education. And I loved those classes immensely. I found Japanese to be so exotic, and after 8 years of French, I jumped at the chance for a change. As for PE, well, I have four older brothers and two older sisters, all of whom are very athletic, so I grew up doing sports. Plus, we had a pretty full house (I have eight siblings), so my mom would often shoo us outside during the day. I did a lot of running around back then.

My worst subject was math. No question. Numbers hate me.

What is your favorite book?

I have a lot of books that come to mind when I think of favorites, but if I had to pick one, it would be *The Count of Monte Cristo* by Alexandre Dumas. It was just the most remarkable revenge story I've ever read, and it was made all the more incredible when I learned Mr. Dumas based the story on real events. I want to travel to Marseille, France, one of these days, just to see Château D'If in person. I'm sure it won't be as remarkable as I imagine it to be, so few places are, but one of these days, I'll get there.

As far as recent children's books, I highly recommend anything by Kenneth Oppel. His *Skybreaker* series is a personal favorite.

What is your favorite travel spot?

I talk about travel a lot, and for that reason, I often get that question. It's really tough to answer since each place I've been has given me something different. Cambodia, for example, is easily one of the most beautiful countries I've ever seen and also one of the saddest. Plus, Angkor Wat is just flat-out spectacular. It remains a bit off the beaten path for most travelers, but I suspect true adventurers won't regret the extra effort it takes to get there.

But if I had to pick one country that just, as a whole, blew me away, I would pick Italy. Beautiful. Historic. Epic. Breathtaking. Friendly. Delicious... These are just some of the words that sum up that country.

Any advice for new writers?

Read lots. Write lots. Learn as much about the industry as you can. That's it. I wish I could give more advice, but the truth is, I'm not qualified. There are far more successful authors out there who have great advice for writers. There are also industry professionals who have blogs and websites dedicated to helping new authors navigate the profession. Oh, and check your sources. Just because everyone is saying something doesn't make it true.

Any final words for your readers?

Yes. I'd like to say THANK YOU! Without the support of readers, I simply couldn't do what I do, and I just want to thank each and every one of you for the support you've given by reading this book. And if you enjoyed it, one of the best things you can do is give it a review or tell a friend about it. Also, if you enjoyed *Glimpse* please pick up a copy of *Relic*, which is book two in the **Dean Curse Chronicles** and will be available by July.

Thank you again, and happy reading!

ABOUT THE AUTHOR

Steven Whibley has lived in British Columbia, Alberta, and Japan; volunteered in Thailand, Myanmar, and Columbia; explored the ruins of Tikal, Angkor Wat, and Cappadocia; and swum with sharks in Belize. The only thing he loves more than traveling the globe and exploring new cultures is writing books (and spending time with his wife and two year old son, Isaiah, of course). Whibley is the seventh of nine children, and uncle to 30 nieces and nephews (and counting).

77683052R00139